SALT RIVER TIMES

WILLIAM MAYNE

SALT RIVER TIMES

GREENWILLOW BOOKS
New York

Library of Congress Cataloging in Publication Data
Mayne, William (date)   Salt River times.
Summary: Twenty-one interlocking stories
about the lives of the people in a small
community along Australia's Salt River.
1. Children's stories, English. [1. Australia—
Fiction. 2. Short stories] I. Title.
PZ7.M4736Sal   [Fic]   80-20806   ISBN 0-688-80311-3

TO JIM AND
EILEEN HAMILTON

CONTENTS

SALT RIVER TIMES

CHAPTER 1

SALT RIVER TIMES

AN OLD WOMAN is telling a story. She says it happened long ago, and she has had a cold ever since. Her nose runs on cold days, so there is a drop on the end of it now. She leaves it there.

Mel is listening. He has his hands in his pockets. He has some gum in his mouth. While he listens he blows a bubble with it like a child. The gum is cold when it gets back in his mouth. Mrs. Anghelidas, who is standing close by, looks at him like he was a monster, so he blows her another bubble. The new bubble isn't so good and gets up his nose. There's the old lady with her drop like water and there's Mel with a big pink one.

Mel gets it in again and goes on waiting for the tram with Joe and Kev, going up to the park and play footy, Kev has the ball. And there's the old woman and Mrs. Anghelidas. The old woman is talking to Mrs. Anghelidas.

"This was out of town when I was young," she says. "Just a paddock. Where we're standing was just a paddock."

Mel thinks that can't be true, because there's a Safeway one side of the road and McDonald's the other, and there must always be something there first. And what's a tram doing in a paddock? But the old woman is saying something about that.

"Before the trams," she said. "Before there were trams here or in the city."

No one is older than a tram, Mel thinks. He wants to tell Joe and Kev about it, and they are talking to each other. Mel thinks the trams are so old you can't believe, so how about someone older than that? Impossible. No one is that old. They wouldn't be alive if they were. But the old woman is, and she's older still.

"There wasn't a school in those days," she says. Mel knows there is something wrong now. They had schools before they had Australia. But the old woman puts it right.

"I had to go to the city each day," she says. Then she

is talking for a bit on how far it was in those days, and Mel is wondering how they learned to talk in those days, that long ago there weren't any words.

Then he stops thinking about that, and Joe stops talking to Kev and listens too, and Kev even stops bouncing the ball on the tram track so the noise won't get in the words.

"I used to pick flowers down by the river," the old woman is saying. "They used to grow there then. I would take them in to school with me on the steamer. The steamer went four times a day from the wharf on the Salt River, down the Salt River and up Hobson's River to the city."

The tram comes. Most times Mel and the others would get on, right, never mind the rest, there's two doors. But today Mel stands about, and Joe won't shove, and Kev lines up after them, and they let the old woman on. Like they'd got manners, Mel thinks. Then they sit near her and go on listening. If you say it on a tram it's public, isn't it?

They have never heard of people going to the city in a steamer, down one river and up the next. Now you can get a train or a bus, or take a tram to Iramoo and change there.

Now what's she saying? The tram's rattling along, all that noise. The old woman speaks like being in a room with you.

"One day we just go in Hobson's River," she is saying.

"We had just turned, right out in the middle because the tide was going out . . ."

Then a big semi comes up beside the tram. You can't hear the old woman now, but Mrs. Anghelidas goes on looking like listening. The semi driver sits up with his elbows on his steering wheel and his engine roars. The old woman's story gets run down, you can't hear it.

Then the tram stops to let people on, and Mel can just hear the pump under the floor, and then that stops. The old woman is still telling her story.

"Well, I heard the captain swear," she says. "And we went down Hobson's River backwards. Stern first. And we should have been going up it, forwards. And down we went, and down we went. It was all green fields down the river then. All green, with trees. No one onshore knew our engine had stopped. But they blew the whistle, and they blew it. All the birds flew up, pelicans, and gulls and cranes. They didn't like the noise."

Then Mel didn't like the noise, because they had come to the lights and got alongside the semi again. Same driver got his elbows on the wheel, looking in front like a dog. Noise in the tram like being in the engine. The lights change, and the semi pulls away. The engine gets quieter. The old woman is talking about engines. She wouldn't know about engines, would she?

She knows a bit. "They'd stopped," she says. "No more go in them. That's why we drifted downstream.

We got up against a mudbank by Stony Creek, where the new bridge is, and we all sat down. Couldn't help it, the boat tipped up. The captain's tea came out of the window, cup and pot and all, and slid down in the water. And there we stuck. She got her bottom on the bank and we got ours on the deck. And there we stopped. They came and pulled us off before long, and back up to the wharf, and I didn't get to school the rest of the week until they fixed it."

"Did you get stuck in the mud a week?" says Kev. You don't need a semi in your ear to help Kev get it wrong. They got off the mud that day. But the old woman doesn't mind he gets it wrong.

"I stayed home a week," she says. "On the farm, down on Hope Street. The block where the Commonwealth Bank is. That was our yard. You still go to school?"

"Got to," says Kev.

"The last day I went," says the old woman, "I never got there."

"We're going to leave before that," says Kev. "Get on a mudbank the day before, we will."

"Your friend reminds me," said the old woman, looking at Joe.

"I never did it," said Joe. "I didn't."

But the old woman hasn't said what he did, so it wasn't wrong. She goes on about her last day. Mel shouts them all tickets, just going up the park and play footy.

"It was foggy on the water," she says. "The air was cold but the water was warm."

"On the steamer?" says Mel.

"On the steamer," she says. "Same steamer, the *Iramoo*. It was a paddle steamer. You could lean over the side and see the wheels go round, and if you fell in you got made into butter, that was the end. We got off the wharf and out on the Salt River. The captain put a bit of bite in the paddles because the tide was coming upstream and we wanted to go down. There was a wind up the river too, with the fog. I don't think the captain knew where he was. But just as we came out of the fog there was a sailing boat coming up straight for us, just along my side. I was there looking at the water and the paddle, like a nong."

Then she stopped. "Will you ring the bell for me?" she asks Kev.

"Yeah," says Kev, and pulls the cord. The bell dings by the driver and the tram stops. This time it gets ahead of the semi, which has to wait back.

"I'll have to tell you the rest another time," she says. "I get off here."

Mel thinks, We shan't see her again, it's only been once in a hundred years so far. If we want to know the end of her time at school. "We get off here, too," he says. "We got to today."

So they get off with her, and stand in the road until she points in the direction of the pavement. Mrs. Anghelidas stays on the tram. Mel blows a big bubble of gum. He knows there will be trouble soon, with Joe and Kev, when they see they have got off before the park.

"There, boys, thank you," says the old woman, setting off for the pavement. The semi driver sits with his elbows on the steering wheel and looks out above them all, like a dog-faced baboon.

"What about your last day at school?" says Mel.

"I was really telling this boy," says the old woman, looking at Joe. "The sailing boat, and you see it was a Chinese one and perhaps they knew no better, came right along the side of the *Iramoo*, and ran right under the paddle-wheel and there was such a bump, and the wheel stopped, and that was lucky, because the next thing I knew I had fallen off the steamer and into the water."

"We better go to the side of the road," says Mel, because the tram had gone but the semi was still waiting and the driver was looking down at them worse than a dog, no wonder.

So they got the old woman to the side of the road, and she told them how the water was warm, and how the Chinamen had pulled her up out of it and put her in their boat. And how they would not stop at the wharf but went up on the tide, up and up, out of the Salt River and into the Iramoo River. And how she sat shivering.

"And so dirty," she says. "The sweet water in the Iramoo River is one thing. But in those days the Salt River was the dirtiest in the state. It must have been. My blue dress was black. I was ashamed of wearing it. And it was full of water. I wanted to get home, but they went up and up the river. I thought I was being kidnapped. I thought I was going for a slave.

"I was quite excited," says Miss White. "I've often wished it had happened. Nothing much else has."

"We thought you were going to say it had," says Mel. "Kind of end the story."

"No ending much," says Miss White. "When that didn't happen. They'd got a market garden up the river, the other side of the trestle bridge. They sailed up there. They had the rest of them up there, and a fire, and they lent me a blanket and I took off my dress in a hut. Then they filled the boat up with vegetables and we went down the river again. They kept my dress, and I didn't know what they were saying. I just had the blanket. And then it was mad. They hung all these vegetables and flowers on me, bunches of carrots, beans, onions, parsley, their kind of cabbage, ginger roots, daisies, all hung on me like a garland."

"They were just going to make you carry them," says Mel. "You did get to be a slave."

"No," says Miss White. "When they'd hung enough radishes and beans on me they took the boat to the wharf and took me to my father's house. He got very angry. He had to buy all the vegetables they'd hung on me. And the next day one of the women brought my dress round, all washed and ironed. It must have taken them hours. They didn't get much thanks from my father. He was that sort of man. In fact he had it in for the Chinese after that, when they had that bit of trouble, and I don't think it got cleared up how the man went missing. But I don't know what went on because I went to school interstate and when I came back I think they'd gone."

"Maybe," says Joe. He's one of them still.

"There's you still," said Miss White. "You could be another lot. But that's a long time later. Now is a long time later than then."

"Maybe," says Joe again, and then he turns his back a bit on Mel and Kev and walks on a bit with the old woman, she gets him by the arm, she's got nothing against Chinese.

While Joe's along there with her Kev looks round. "Hey, will you look at that?" he says. "We're worse off than we started, Mel. We've got away past the park and we'll have to walk back and it's further than when we began, and we paid to do it."

"You don't need me to get off a tram," says Mel. "Come on, Joe, we're waiting for you."

"O.K.," says Joe, and gets away from the old woman.

"She was just telling me that she knows it isn't tinned cat food at the take-away."

"You got to believe something," says Mel.

"Hey," says Joe, because he's begun to notice too. "You got us off the tram about nine blocks late. We get to walk now, do we?"

"Yeah," says Mel. "No worries though. I'll shout you the walk. Right?"

"Right on," says Kev, it suits him, something free. Joe says something else. It could be a Chinese word, if you don't know anything better. So they think up some other words for themselves, and walk back to the park gates hanging the words round their shoulders like Miss White's vegetables. But hers were all good fresh vegetables. These are all old bad words.

CHAPTER 2

SEA SERPENT

"What you come in so late for?" said Gwenda's mother. "So late, much too late, coming home from school this time."

"Just coming home from school," said Gwenda. "It's where I was, isn't it?"

"Don't you be cheeky to me, my girl," said her mother. "Where you go coming from school, eh? I look out and you don't come and you don't come and then you come the other way, and home is here, not some other house."

"I just came round by the river," said Gwenda.

"You keep away from dirty place like the river," said her mother. "Dirty water in the river and all the rubbish been there years and years."

"I didn't say I went in it," said Gwenda. "Just on the road, just on the bank."

"Well, I don't like it," said her mother. "You come home from school a better way."

But Gwenda did not take much notice. She walked that way with Sophia sometimes, that was all. She went that way the next day, and the next day after that, but she was not really friends with Sophia every day.

The next day after that, Thursday, Sophia had got tired of her, because really Gwenda treated every friend in the way she treated her mother. No one liked her for four days in a row.

On Thursday she had fallen out with Sophia so she went along by the river alone. It was not a dirty river, she thought. Of course there was mud in it. You get mud if you mix water and earth. You get water and earth if you mix rivers with land. And the other way about.

In fact the river was cleaner than coffee. Or Gwenda was thinking that before she looked. She had thought how clean it was when she went down the gravel road to the water. She was going to walk along the bank behind the houses, just by the water. This was the way she came with Sophia. When they were together Gwenda was busy making Sophia agree with her about things. She had no time to look where she was going.

Now she thought she would look at the river and find it was clean and make her mother agree. She knew she must be right, because she had thought of it so clearly.

The river hadn't been thinking clearly. It was the color of coffee. But coffee does not have things floating in it and on it. On the water there was slimy green oil. In the water were lumps that looked like bundles of toes or ears, going black. At the edge of the water there was half of a car engine, red and black with rust. Beside it was a heap of ash, and all round were beer cans. On the bank and in the water were plastic wrappers and bags and pieces.

There was mud. It was covered in green slime. Bubbles came up out of it. They burst, and had a bad smell.

There was a small dead fish hanging in the water. Nothing moved. All the nasty things stayed where they were.

There were lumps of brick by a garden fence. Gwenda threw one at the floating fish. She missed it, but it wobbled, at least. Then it was all still again. Nothing moved by the bank.

She looked out across the water. The other bank was nearly the same. Gwenda thought she had lost. Her mother would not agree with her now that the river was clean. It was not. The best thing was to keep quiet about it. Perhaps, she thought, if I waited a few days and then shouted at her that the river was dirty, then she would have to agree with me. That is not the same as me agreeing with her.

So she felt that she had not lost. She picked up a good big piece of brick and threw it into the middle of the river. To teach it a lesson.

The water rippled. And something out there in the middle lifted up its head and looked at her. It looked first with one eye, and turned round and looked with the other.

Then it put its head under the water and began to swim up the river. Its head came up and looked at her again.

Most people would have gone home then.

Gwenda picked up another brick and threw it. She picked up another, ready.

The head looked at her again. It went on swimming up the river. Behind it was a long body that showed above the water in little lumps. It was very long. The whole thing was a monster of some sort.

Most people would have gone home by now, at least.

Gwenda threw her third brick. She hit the thing in the middle of its back. It shook its head and stopped swimming.

Gwenda walked up the bank, level with its head. All she did before she walked was see that she knew the way back. Most people would have left, but she just took care.

The thing was going to have to agree with her.

But it took no more notice. It looked at her with one eye only. It rocked its head a little, and that was all.

Then it went on up the river. Gwenda watched it go. She let it go for today, and went home for tea. On her way she got her foot in the water, because the tide was rising and lifting the river.

Her mother shook her for that, and told her never to go to the river again.

But Gwenda went on Friday after school and saw the monster swimming further down. She shouted at it to come back. But she was at the back of Sophia's house, and only Sophia answered by looking over the fence. But they did not speak to each other. And the monster said nothing.

On Saturday she walked a long way up the bank, until she came to the high wall at the tallow factory. There was nowhere to walk, and the smell was worse than she could remember after. The monster was not up there. She walked down the river to the wharfs and went home.

"Where have you been?" said her mother. "You smell. Smell."

"You live here too," said Gwenda.

But it was the tallow factory smell, in her hair, and she had to have it washed.

On Sunday she thought, No one likes me for four

days, so they don't hate me for four days. So the monster will come today.

And all the morning she knew it was waiting for her, but her mother kept her in the house. And in the afternoon her uncle came and stayed and stayed.

Then, with the beer and television, they all fell asleep and she could go out. She went down to the water.

The river was down low. The tide was out and all the mud was drying. There was a nasty smell, and a dead dog, and the mud was thick.

Out in the middle of the mud, in the middle of the river, looking for her, was the monster. There was not enough water to swim.

So she had only to wait. She knew he would swim to her.

And that would have been all right. But the other side of the river were two boys. They had a rope with a noose on it. They were trying to throw the noose over the monster's head.

"It's mine. Stop it," shouted Gwenda.

"Get lost," said one boy.

"Rack off," said the other.

If they had been sensible they would have gone home. For one thing they were messing with a monster in the river. For another, they did not know Gwenda. If they had they would have gone.

First she threw stones and bricks at them. The half

bricks were too heavy. Smaller pieces were better. She could just get them across the water. And she was a good shot. She had practiced on Sophia.

The boys did not take much notice of that. By the time the stones got across the river they had nearly stopped moving.

Gwenda grew tired of throwing. Her arm ached. She made a different sort of attack. She ran up into the road, down it to the bridge by the wharf, and across the bridge. She could still see the boys from the bridge.

Then she got down on the riverbank on their side. They thought she had gone away. But she had not. She was angry enough for six. She gathered stones and pieces of iron and some tough mud. She took her stones and iron and mud up behind a wall.

Then she waited.

She thought the boys might as well do the work for her. She gave them time and they did it.

After a great many throws they got their noose over the head of the monster and started to pull it in. She let them pull it.

Really, before, she had been thinking that the monster was alive, and alive for her. But now she did not care about that. She would rather have a fight than a friend. And she knew the monster was something floating up and down the river on the salty tide. But he belonged to her.

And when the boys had brought him across the mud and were about to put their hands on him she started the fight.

The boys ran away. Most boys would have run away much earlier. But these did not know her.

They ran away. They dropped their rope and yelled and ran. Gwenda threw some stones after them and then ran down to the monster.

The monster was a piece of wood. She had been right. It was a monster, a head carved from wood, with eyes that had some gold on them, and teeth that were broken but had some white on them. The long tail was a trailing rope with canvas and cloth and weed on it.

She put her arms around the head, just touching with her hands. The smell was very bad. But she knew she had to drag the monster home.

Then the boys came back. Everything went wrong for Gwenda. She took hold of the monster and mud covered her arms. She tried to run away, because she had no stones to throw. She ran into the mud of the river. She tripped over the rope and fell down, and the head fell asleep on her and knocked all her breath out.

So the boys rescued her.

"It's a little kid of about nine," said one. His name was Mel.

"Yeah," said the other, whose name was Kev. "We'll take her back to her home."

"We'll drop her back in the river," said Mel.

But they picked her up and carried her home, and after them they dragged the wooden head, and they put them both in at her gate and left her.

Anyone else would have run away then. But not Gwenda. She was brave. She knew there would be trouble. But she walked up to the door, opened it.

"I fell in the river," she said. "It is very dirty."

"I should throw you back," said her mother kindly. "Just rubbish in that river, you know, just rubbish."

CHAPTER 3

BLACKBIRDS

IN THE NIGHT the town seemed to go away. All the traffic fell silent, and no noise came from the houses. Joe was woken by the quiet.

He was lying there listening and hoping for a sound, hoping for something to tell him he was awake, alive, and still where he lived.

There was nothing to hear. There was nothing to see. All the lamps in the street had gone out. All the light from the houses had gone.

Joe thought that he had woken into nowhere and

nothing, or perhaps was still asleep in nowhere and nothing.

He knew he was not frightened. But it was a strange night to be around in. It was a strange night to have round him. He was about to tell himself to go to sleep again when the sounds began.

Something called out of the sky. Joe told himself it was a train. But it was not. The call came again, and was answered, like a trumpet blowing, and coming more and more so that a tune formed.

Joe sat up to hear it better. It must be police cars far away in the city, their sirens carrying in the still night. But he knew it was not that.

He was wide awake now. He could see the shape of his window, and the sky across the top of it. There was a touch of early morning light in it, and the end of the moonlight.

The trumpets grew quieter, but did not go far away. Next there was a whistling that came gently from all around, and with the whistling there were grunts and calls and cries. Overhead, somewhere in the air, there was a heavy treading of wings and something flew across the house, something that took a long time to pass by.

Joe got up and out of bed, jumping into his trousers without looking what he was doing, pulling on a skivvy without thinking, shoving on his shoes without feeling in the dark. His heart had begun to flap. The thing overhead, what was it?

Then he sat down on the bed and took some deep breaths. He had at last had the sense to look outside. There, against the lightness of the sky he could see what there was. A great flock of birds was circling the town, and he had heard their great number of wings beating, low over the houses.

He thought he would go out. But his feet felt strange and his trousers would not zip up. Also his skivvy had gone mad and had only one sleeve and a collar of large size. So he had to stop and sort all that out.

The trousers were on back to front. The feet were in the wrong shoes. And the skivvy had one sleeve inside the other.

He got the clothes right and went outside.

The air was full of birds. Now and then one or two landed on a rooftop, but they soon picked themselves off with a call and flew after their mates.

There were more kinds than Joe could tell. But he could pick out the swans by their necks, the pelicans by their size, and spoonbills by the shape of their bills.

All of them were circling above the houses and their wings made more noise than their voices, except when the swans called like trumpets.

Joe went down the street and towards the Salt River. These were water birds, he knew. The river was where they would mostly be.

He was slightly wrong. But the birds he had seen were only part of the thousands there that morning.

Once, beyond the Salt River, between the town of
Iramoo and the city, all the land had been a swamp
where birds gathered. But in these days the docks and
warehouses had grown over that swamp. The birds had
remembered the land as it once was, and had come back
to it and found there was nothing left.

There was nowhere for them, nowhere to settle, nowhere to take fish and frogs.

Joe stood by the river and saw beyond it how the
birds skimmed low and heard them lift up again with
despairing cries and circle again and again, dark shapes
against the hard dry roads and buildings that covered
their homeland.

Joe was not alone. He saw a girl standing further
along the bank of the river. He knew who she was,
though he had never spoken to her. He had heard a
sound that was not the birds. It was the girl, and she
was looking at them too, and crying gently at the sadness of it.

Joe did not know why she was crying. He thought he
should cheer her up. He had a thought that cheered him
up. He thought that if he had a gun he could shoot a
great many birds. He thought that idea would appeal to
the girl. But when he came closer to her she looked at
him and said, "Don't tell anyone," she said. "They will
come and kill as many as they can. You must not tell
anyone."

She was so upset that Joe knew he was wrong to

think of shooting. "Sure, Elissa," he said. "I was just looking." Of course that was true. He thought she was being a little strange about a few birds.

"Just birds," he said, kindly.

"Oh, yes," said Elissa. "They will die because of all the roads and docks. But what if it happened to you?"

"Well, it wouldn't," said Joe.

"Well, it could," said Elissa. "It happened to my father and his family before he came to Australia."

"But not here," said Joe.

"Come with me," said Elissa. "You will see I am not all in tears about the birds only. There are some other things. But because it is only birds you do not think of the other things. Come along up the river to the park. Come along."

By then Joe had begun to feel cold. He did not want to go along the riverbank, in the dark, to any other place. There was nothing he could do for the birds that still circled above him. In fact he had an idea they were circling higher and beginning to fly away.

"This is not a real night," said Elissa. Joe wondered whether it was a real night. "These are not real birds," she said, and Joe wondered whether he could see through some of the shadowy shapes, whether the birds were flying through walls and power poles. "This is one of those strange nights. Come along please," she said.

And she took his hand and pulled him along. Joe

shivered from the cold of the night and from the cold
of her hand. But he did not let go.

She took him along the riverbank where the salt
water lapped at the grass, and to the edge of the park.
"Now," she said. "See by the water. They have been
there all night, coming and going, like the birds."

Joe looked. He was expecting to see more birds, and
that was what he tried to see, birds standing in the
water. Then he saw he was looking at people.

Those thin legs were not legs. They were the shafts of
spears. These were men, not birds.

"Those are abos," he said.

"Shush," said Elissa.

"Black people," said Joe. "Blackbirds, not black
swans."

"They will hear," said Elissa. "We should not be
found watching. They could kill you, because you have
sent them away from their home, like the birds. Black
people will not love white people."

"Oh," said Joe. "I'm Chinese in the daytime. But I
never did anything to them. Or the birds, either."

"You will build a house one day," said Elissa. "On
their land."

"Now you hush," said Joe, because she was speaking
loudly. "They'll hear you."

"I do not know that they are real," said Elissa. "This
is all my dream, perhaps."

Perhaps it was the dream of the black people too. They were dark against the ground, but not dark enough to be quite real. It was easy for Joe to see that they were moving in some sort of dance, and if he listened he could hear something that might be singing and drumming and the muttering of other things. But his looking always melted what he was looking at, and his hearing only heard things further away.

"You will build a house too, one day," he said, at last, when his eyes and ears could only buzz.

"That is why I cry for them," said Elissa. "I shall be as bad as anyone. I shall do what people in another country did to my grandfather."

"They're only shadows down there," said Joe.

"Of course," said Elissa. "The people that were here have died, and the birds that come here still die. We were very wicked. Can you give them back to themselves? Can you give them the land again, land for the people, the swamp for the birds?"

"Well," said Joe, "I didn't want to have this dream and get into all this strife. So I want to go home and get back to bed and wake up."

"Then you will let go of my hand, please," said Elissa.

"Get back on the road first," said Joe.

"Ha," said Elissa. "Then you do feel there is danger and wickedness."

"No way," said Joe, but they both knew that was not true. He felt guilty and frightened.

"Good night," said Elissa, when they came up to the

road again and she took her hand back. "Be seeing you."

"No way," said Joe again, but he said it to himself.

On the way home the birds still cried overhead. And at many a corner, beyond many a power pole, behind the telephone box, against fences, in trees, against awnings, in shop doors, he thought he saw the shadow of the first men, the straight stroke of the spear, the glistening of an eye. They were there against the other shadows, but as the light came up they faded as they walked out of the town. And in the same way the birds left the swamp that was no longer there when the cars and buses and semis began to fill the roads and the goods and work began to fill the harsh stone wharves.

Joe went to sleep, or went on sleeping. He did not know which, whether he had woken or had a dream with no meaning. But he wondered what he would re-member of Iramoo and whether he would come back.

Later, in the park, going up to play footy, he found the nest of a little blackbird in an English tree growing by the water, where she had her eggs, home from home.

CHAPTER 4

SHOW AND TELL

Sir says to me, "Good day, Morgan."

I say to him, "Good day, Sir," and he smiles, and smiles, and I smile and he smiles, and I smile and I smile, and he goes on down the yard.

But my smile grows and grows, wider and wider, and my teeth stretch and I bite off his head, and his body, and his knees, crunch, crunch, crunch.

But he forgets and goes on walking into school. And I stop being the school snake, but I'll be something else next, and another thing later. They aren't going to get away.

Now what is greasy Gwenda bringing in? A big lump of wood, that's what. She's got a rope round it and she's dragging it in the gate.

It's got eyes. It's got eyes on it. It's a head. It's a snake's head. It's me, she's dragging me. I'm going to tell her to put me down.

But my mouth is full of mud. I see it when I run over to Gwenda.

"Get off it," she says. "Rack off," and she hits me with the rope end just on the knee. Snakes don't have knees, so it doesn't hurt. It hurts somebody, but not me, and that person is lying on the ground. Snakes lie on the ground, so perhaps it's me.

Greasy Gwenda pulls my head away and bangs it on the wall. I don't feel it much. She kicks it on the cheek. I turn into a hole in the ground, just behind her.

It's no good being a snake with Gwenda around the place. You'd die. So I'm a hole now.

Gwenda kicks the head again. It's a piece of wood now. I'm a piece of wood as well as a hole, that's it. Now she turns the tap on. No one's allowed to turn the tap on. I hope all the water doesn't run down the hole that's me.

It doesn't. The water goes down the yard. But Gwenda falls in the hole, and guess what, the snake got her, and she's dead.

But the hole ran away, and she went into school. So I was the next thing, a big tree with a clock in it so it knows when it's time to go in.

It can't get in the door because of the branches, so I have to go in and get a saw from the art room and saw the branches off until Sir takes it away and says, "Get in there," so it's just the clock that goes in, all these numbers written on my face. I can feel them, but no good looking in the mirror because I don't know when the clock's right because it gets different again.

Then I change into water. There's water coming under the door before I change. I change into it. I try hot and I try cold. Cold is right. There's a little bit of me under the door, but outside, where they can't see, is the whole sea, and I splash out everywhere, all these ships on me.

And I go trickling in under the door, that's the hard part. I'm so big I have to squash flat to get there. But I'm reaching out and reaching out, and I get to a nail in the floor, and I get to a bit of wool and it floats. The nail doesn't. It's fixed in the floor. And I get to a crack.

No one else sees it. I'm going to bring it up and up and up until Sir is standing on the desk and all the kids are in up to their necks, and then I'll pop up over their heads and get Sir's shoes wet.

But when I tried and tried there was only still a puddle under the door, all real. Outside there's the sea.

Then Mr. Hill gets going outside, head teacher. All

my sea out there dries up when he yells.

All the chalk dries up on the board, and the drawings fall off. But that doesn't stop him.

All the windows turn to sky and the birds fly in and out. But that doesn't stop him.

I make a big island in the sea with a lion on top of it. But that doesn't stop him.

"Who turned that tap on?" he yells. It isn't just him, of course, but a fleet of whales. I can tell. He'll come under the door in a minute.

"Is it somebody in here?" says Sir.

Then Mr. Hill comes in. He doesn't come under the door. He opens it, and of course all the sea pours in with him, all the whales and the lion. He swims in and the lion goes out of the window.

Gwenda changed into those things you can't see. She thinks she isn't there, but you can tell there's something greasy.

"I'll turn it off," says Sir, because he can't see Gwenda either, so he knows who it is.

"I know it's someone in here," says Mr. Hill. "I won't have it, I won't have the tap turned on, you aren't to touch it," and shouting it.

I turn the knobs on my desk to switch him off, who wants channel two? So he has an advertisement or two about the water under the door and goes away. Nothing about the sea outside, but that's private.

"Saved your life, Gwenda," says Sir. Gwenda blows

her nose. I try to make her head come off in the tissue but it won't. It's the grease.

"What is it?" says Sir. Gwenda says it's her show and tell. So we start our show and tell. I've got this bouncing diamond, but I don't want to show it.

First we get Darren. He went up the river fishing with his dad. I'd catch a lot more than that because he didn't catch anything. He shows us the hook he didn't do it with, and it gets caught in our throats and he takes it out with a thing he's got and we bleed to death on the bank.

Then there's Katie. "Mr. Bryce, boys and girls," she says, but she doesn't say me because I'm a machine pumping the river full, then I'm pumping mountains until I've got it all fixed.

Katie brings all these little wisps of hair off her granny and her auntie and her mum and her brother. The one we can't see is off her grandad because he's got no hair. There's a bit off her dog, and off her cat, and off the budgie, the one she calls a leaf from the fur of a bird.

Sophia has a great big dead spider. She says it died in their house. But it creeps off her hand and gets bigger and bigger and sits in a chair, and then it takes Paul and begins to eat him, and Paul hasn't enough legs so it takes Bindi and Alex. Then Sophia puts it away and they stop being eaten.

Then Sir goes out and gets Gwenda's thing in the rubbish bin and puts it on the table. Gwenda says it

was swimming up and down the river and she got it out.
She says it looked at her.

It looks at Sir now, and it turns him into a stone. It
looks at Gwenda and she turns into lard. She says it's
the fossil of a dinosaur. Dead.

But I think it's alive. It could give rides. My desk
turns to a motorcycle and I go up the wall over the
blackboard and across the ceiling and down the other
side. You can stay on the ceiling if you go fast enough.
Sir says the bike is making too much noise so I cross on
the red light and run him over nine times. But he just
writes dinosaur on the board, and Darren says the smell
makes him sick.

But he won't have the flying doctor on the motor-
bike come to see him. So Sir puts the head outside, and
I make Sophia's spider spin all this web over the door
and he can't get in again, but he does. Nothing gets
outside my head. But Sir says nothing gets in either.

When school gets out there's Mr. Hill in the yard
and the wooden head looks at him and he looks back
at it, and I fly round him like a bat eating blowflies and
motorbikes making the same noise.

Gwenda walks past the head. She won't take it with
Mr. Hill watching. No way, she says. I say I'll carry it
for her if she'll let me keep it. It's got jewel eyes, that's
why it can look at you. Gwenda says just carry it to the
street, but I'm not going to just do that.

I turn Mr. Hill deaf and dumb so I don't hear what

he says, but I should just have done him blind. I make the eyes look at him. Then I pick up and turn into a snake and the teeth eat him up, right to the knees, and I go out of the other gate and ride the snake home before greasy Gwenda can get near, and when she does I haven't got it.

It got heavy. It turned itself to stone. I put it in a garden. Gwenda turns me to stone, but I don't feel it, because I don't know when she hits me. Then I turn back into a hole in the ground but she jumps in me and I have to come out of there. And I smile and I stretch my teeth to eat her but she bites my tongue with them. And I get to give her the head back. It was still in the garden.

So nothing happened today.

CHAPTER 5

FORGIVING

ONE DAY Ivan came up to Joe and punched him on the arm. You can do that to a friend and he doesn't mind. You can do it to an enemy and it hurts him.

"What's that for?" said Joe. He did not know which he was, friend or enemy.

"Keep off my sister," said Ivan. "That's what it's for."

"I don't know your sister," said Joe.

"You do so," said Ivan. "My uncle saw you."

"Not me," said Joe. "I'm fussy. I wouldn't go near any sister of yours."

Ivan hit the other arm.

"Watch it," said Joe. "I'm telling you, mate."

Mel was there too. "You heard him, Ivie," he said. "He never saw your sister, and doesn't want to."

"My uncle," said Ivan, but he didn't get far this time.

"We didn't know you had an uncle, even," said Mel. "You give him a kiss for his sister, Joe, and I'll give him one for his uncle." They were going to be kisses with the fist. Ivan ran away.

"You were in the park with her at five in the morning," he said. "Holding hands. Keep off her."

"He wasn't. Get lost," said Mel.

"Keep off," Ivan shouted. "Dirty Chinaman." By then he had got quite away. Mel wanted to go after him, but Joe said it was not worth the trouble. If people didn't like him being Chinese he would put up with it. Then the buzzer went for the next lesson.

"Later," said Mel.

"See you," said Joe.

The next day was a holiday, so they didn't see Ivan. The day after was Saturday. Both days Joe worked at the shop. Mel did nothing.

He and Joe met up on Saturday night. They went down to Kev's house for a bit and watched a replay on TV. Mel tried to telephone home and say he would be late but someone was using it at home. Then he forgot about it.

So it was late when Mel and Joe left Kev's. It was

very late. It was all right for Joe. He had got through to
his house. But Mel had not tried again. They hurried
along the streets.

They didn't get home very soon at all.

"There's Ivan," said Joe suddenly. "I've got to tell
him something." He wanted to tell Ivan that he had met
Ivan's sister, and it was at five in the morning, in the
park, but that it was only by accident. He had only remembered now by seeing Ivan hurrying along another
street, just like the people he had seen on his way home
the other time. That had reminded him.

"She's a funny kid," he said. "She thinks we're all
terrible just for being alive. Let's catch up with him and
give him a fright and tell him he was right after all."

"I don't know what you were doing with his sister,"
said Mel. "What were you doing?"

"Nothing," said Joe. "I woke up and went for a walk,
and there she was."

"He called you a dirty Chinaman," said Mel.

"Forget it," said Joe. "We'll just give him a fright
and won't tell him he's right."

"Who'd want to be right about his sister?" said Mel.
But all the time he meant to hit Ivan twice, because he
knew Joe would never manage it. Joe was too easy about
things.

They ran up the street after Ivan. Ivan looked round
and hurried on. He did not need to run yet.

"Where does he live?" said Joe.

"Down by the Salt River," said Mel. "Right on it. Look, now we've got him running."

"He isn't going home," said Joe.

"Might be going the long way," said Mel. "He'll turn right up at the top. If he goes straight on he gets to the railway buildings and he can't get out. We'll have him then."

"Aw, come on, leave it," said Joe. "See him some other time, not the middle of the night."

"O.K.," said Mel. "No, wait a minute. Look what he's doing, the dill. He's gone straight up the street. He can't get away now."

"We'll just walk up and get him," said Joe, changing his mind. "We'll just walk up to him. I'll have to hit him for being so helpful."

"Then we'll run home," said Mel. "They'll kill me."

Ivan had gone up the dark end of the street. There was no way out, and there was one streetlamp lighting it. They could see him walking up one side. They ran again. He did not seem to hear them coming.

He walked slower and slower. Mel and Joe came quietly along in doorways. Mel thought perhaps they would only give him a scare. But he knew they would hit him as well, even if it would be a bit wrong.

Joe looked at Mel. Mel looked at Joe. Ivan looked at the doorway near him and stood still. Joe nodded. Mel nodded.

Together they jumped forward. But at that moment

Ivan walked forward, opened a door in the wall, and went through.

"Get him," said Mel. Ivan looked round and saw them, because there was light coming out from the doorway. He pushed the door against them, but they pushed against him. They got in there with him.

"Welcome, please come in," said a very fat lady. And she gave each of them a candle, got behind them, and pushed them through another doorway into a hot bright room full of people and smoke and long music.

"It's a temple," said Joe.

"That group singing is sudden death," said Mel. But they were pushed and pulled into the middle of the room, where it was hotter and hotter, and they were being pressed on by so many people standing there with candles in their hands, and the music was so loud, and the smoke so thick, and the light so bright, that they could not get out. And when they looked for the doorway they could not find it.

"It is a temple," said Joe. "Look at all those photographs of God on the wall."

"I can't read the writing," said Mel. "It's the Russian church, Joe. Is that where they cut your dicky off?"

Joe thought that was so funny that he laughed out loud. Several ladies turned round and waved their fingers and hushed him. "Hey," said Joe, "if Ivan's Russian that's why he doesn't like Chinese. That's O.K. then. I thought he was just Australian."

They found they had got to the front of the crowd. They could not go any further because of a railing and because of a big bed of candles burning hotly and sending smoke into their mouths.

Then lights went off and on, and out of a small door beyond the railing came a big, bearded man. He was dressed in robes. He was singing in a great bearlike voice, or perhaps it was a sort of shouting. Mel and Joe did not know the words, but the rest of the people did, and they shouted back.

Then the candles were being lighted all round. Flames were given to Joe and Mel. There was not room to move, but all the people managed it, and made a path down the middle of the church. The man who had shouted went singing and shouting down the path. He was helped by two others, one with a voice like a drum, one with a voice like wood being sawn.

After them came a boy carrying a banner, like a flag. With him were other boys with silver plates on poles. The boy carrying the flag was Ivan.

"That's him," said Joe. Mel said he knew. His candle nearly burned a piece of lace on a fat lady.

After Ivan and the boys came women and girls carrying pictures and books.

"That's her," said Joe. He was pointing to one of the girls. She was carrying a picture. "She's called Elissa."

"You wouldn't want to talk to her," said Mel.

"No way," said Joe.

"And we can't do anything to Ivie," said Mel. "They'd get us if we did."

"Right," said Joe. "How we getting out, Mel?"

It was easy to get out of the church. It just took a little time. Some of the people began following the men and girls, like a parade. Joe and Mel joined in. It seemed to be the right thing to do. They were meant to be singing but they did not know the sounds. Warm wax from the candles ran on their fingers.

A door opened in the end of the church. The parade went through the door and outside. It was colder, and the singing went away on the air.

But there was nowhere to go from here. They were just in a narrow yard. There was another door at the end of the yard and the parade went through that. They were in a street then, but not one that Mel or Joe knew. They stayed with the people.

Another doorway took them into the church again, and they had got out but got in again, and not got away. The men and boys, with Ivan, and the girls, with Elissa, went away behind the railings and there was some more singing.

Mel and Joe could hardly move again. They could not find the first door they had come in at. They had to stay where they were. Mel did not mind, but he knew he should be at home.

The parade began again. Joe and Mel joined in once more. This time they did better, and got out into the street they knew, the one they had followed Ivan up. So, by standing aside at the last moment they got left outside. They were alone at last, holding their burning candles, and hearing the music go on without them.

"I'm off," said Mel. "They'd have killed me at home even if I was earlier than this. I don't know what they'll do now."

So he blew out his candle, and Joe pinched his out.

But they still did not get home. Out of the door there came Ivan, without his flag, but with a candle. He blew out the candle, put it between his teeth, and punched Joe on the arm. It was a friendly punch. Joe just punched him back, even more friendly, and a bit harder.

But that was all. Next there came Elissa, and their little sister Sophia, and their parents, and some uncles and aunts and grandparents.

"These are friends of yours," said Ivan's mother. "Well, that is very nice. I saw them in church. You must come home with us, but first of all," and she came forward and took hold of Mel and kissed him three times. "It is the right thing to do this morning. It is Easter Day," she said. Then she did the same thing to Joe.

"You can kiss my sisters," said Ivan. "If you want."

"We don't want," said Mel. "I got to get home."

"No, no," said Ivan's mother, "first you come to our house for something to eat. It is so long since we had anything, we are so hungry."

"We just came to beat Ivie up," said Mel.

"Oh, that is all forgotten," said Ivan's mother. "You have forgiven him now, haven't you?"

"We forgave him first," said Mel. "But we still had to hit him. But I won't bother. I don't want to. I've got to get home."

But Ivan's mother took hold of him, and a very old lady took hold of Joe. They went to Ivan's house at the edge of the Salt River, and ate eggs, and cakes with domes on, and a bright red salad.

Mel left Joe with the very old lady. The old lady was taking to Joe about toilets. Joe did not mind. Mel had heard old people talking to Joe about toilets before, and one day he was going to ask him why. When he left Joe was talking to the old lady about dragons.

Mel told Ivan that Joe did not care at all about anyone's sister, but mostly he didn't care about Ivan's.

Ivan said he didn't either, most of the time. "But what about Joe and my great-grandma, eh?"

Then Mel got home later than he had ever been. "What's it all about?" said his father. "We weren't worried, just thought you were dead, that's all."

Mel said that was all right, thanks for the thought, and if he'd been dead he'd be up in a day or two because it was Easter. And his dad said that was enough of that, mate, get to bed.

CHAPTER 6

ASHES TO ASHES

ONE DAY Mr. Lee came into River Street and burned down Mr. Young's house.

He did it with a box of matches and some kero.

He came in his ute. Before he burned the house down he went inside and brought out some furniture.

Everybody knew Mr. Young did not have much furniture.

Everybody knew he slept in a chair.

And when he sat down he sat on the floor.

And that his table was like a grade prep table. You could walk on to it, it was so low.

Mr. Lee brought out the chair and the table.

He brought out a red cupboard. He put them on the nature strip.

He brought out a black cupboard.

He brought out a carpet. He put the carpet in the ute, rolled up.

He brought out the kitchen stove. It had fire in it.

He emptied out the fire in the garden and stamped on it until it was black and cold.

No one thought that was strange. They did not know he was going to burn the house down.

Gwenda came to watch.

"Is he dead?" she said. "Is old Mr. Young dead?"

"Don't think so," said Mr. Lee.

Sophia came up to watch. She stayed the other side of the gate from Gwenda. She did not go near Gwenda until Gwenda asked her to. Even then she mostly stayed away. Perhaps Gwenda was not very nice to Sophia. But sometimes the stones she threw at Sophia did not hit, so perhaps she sometimes tried to be nice.

"Is he dead?" said Sophia. "Old Mr. Young?"

Mr. Lee was bringing out a cooking pot.

"He wasn't dead last time he spoke to me," he said.

Morgan came along then. He had Rick with him.

Rick had a rope round his middle to stop him crawling away.

"He died of a fever," said Morgan. "I saw these big germs down here yesterday. They got him."

"Old Mr. Young," said Gwenda.

"Old Mr. Old," said Sophia.

"Young Mr. Old," said Morgan.

Rick said, "Ha ha ha ha ha," and walked into the tree on the nature strip.

Then he sat down.

"I wish she'd had a dog, not a baby," said Morgan. "Then I could put a proper lead on it."

Sophia wondered what sort of germs Morgan had seen.

"Morning germs," said Morgan. "Kill you."

Gwenda said they'd killed old Mr. Young.

Mr. Lee came out with a carved chest.

"You still here?" he said. Then he had a rest from carrying things from the house. He took them from the nature strip and put them in the ute.

Gwenda looked over one side of the ute. Sophia went round and looked over the other.

Morgan and Rick stood at the end. Mr. Lee caught his foot in the rope.

"Now go home," he said. "Get out of the road."

Morgan picked Rick up and put him on his feet.

"If that had been a dog it would have bitten you," he said.

"You and your dog keep out of the ute," said Mr. Lee.

He went into Mr. Young's house for something else.

"If he's dead," said Gwenda. "If he is."

"Of course he is," said Morgan.

"He's in that big chest," said Sophia.

"I don't care where he is," said Gwenda. But she moved away from the chest.

"He's in the carpet," said Morgan. "That's how it's done, they roll them up in a carpet."

Sophia went away from the carpet. It was her side of the ute.

"Listen," said Gwenda. "I don't care where he is." But she would not go near the chest.

"We don't want him," she said. "But he was once a pirate."

Mr. Lee came out with a painted screen.

"Wasn't he once a pirate?" said Gwenda.

"No," said Mr. Lee. "He grew cabbages somewhere up the Iramoo River. Cabbage patch."

"He dug up some treasure," said Sophia. "We know."

"He buried some treasure," said Morgan. "My dad said. It was all in the papers."

"I never heard," said Mr. Lee. "Perhaps he won the golden cabbage one time. But I never heard of that either. Now beat it. There's nothing here for you."

So then he got into the ute and drove off. He had not started to burn the house down yet.

Gwenda and Sophia and Morgan had no idea that he would. Rick was not thinking of anything. Unless he thought he was Morgan's dog.

But he was not making a good job of it. He had not grown long ears, or fur, or a long tail. But he walked on all four legs.

The ute went down River Street and turned a corner.

"If there's a treasure," said Gwenda, "then it's still here. He would have said if he'd taken it."

Sophia thought he might have taken the treasure and said nothing.

But Gwenda wouldn't like her to say so.

"What are you looking like that for?" said Gwenda to Sophia.

Sophia stopped even thinking different from Gwenda.

"Go in the house and get the treasure," said Gwenda.

Sophia thought it was nice of her not to throw a stone or hit her with a stick.

"It's in the cellar," said Morgan. "If you don't go you can't share."

"No one will get it," said Gwenda.

"It'll go rotten," said Morgan. "It gets holes in it, treasure does."

"Everybody knows he's got it," said Gwenda. "Go on, you have to get it for us."

Sophia felt very sad then. Gwenda was being so kind about it. But Sophia did not want to go in the house to look for treasure. She hated the thought. She was frightened of going in.

But Gwenda was being so kind. It would be much easier if Gwenda threw stones or spat or kicked. Then Sophia would have run away.

But she went in at the gate.

The garden didn't feel like a place where there was treasure. It felt there might be snakes.

The veranda didn't feel like a place where there was treasure. It felt there might be spiders.

The door was open. There was an empty room inside. Nothing was there. It did not feel like a place where there was treasure. It felt there might be mice.

She went in. There was another room beyond. It had something in it.

Something making a noise. It was a tap, dripping one drip at a time. It did not feel like a place where there was treasure. It felt there might be damp.

There was another door. She went through that. She was in the backyard. It did not feel like a place where there was treasure. It felt there might be cats. It smelled there might be cats.

There was a door to the alley at the back of the houses. Sophia went through that. She closed it behind her.

And on the other side of the fence, in the yard she

had just left, or in the room with the tap, or in the empty other room, there was a noise.

Someone coughed. And sneezed. And said, "Hrrmph."

Sophia ran away along the alley. She did not know which way to go. She thought she ran both ways. But she only came out at one end, in the next street.

When she came out she saw Mr. Lee's ute going by.

She thought she might be safe with Gwenda if he was there.

She came along to the corner and then along River Street again.

Mr. Lee had gone up to Mr. Young's house and was inside when Sophia came there.

"I didn't find anything," she whispered to Gwenda.

Gwenda was looking over the fence at the house. She had not heard Sophia walk up to her.

She jumped. "You didn't look," she said.

"In the cellar," said Morgan.

"I didn't look there," said Sophia. She knew that if she had it would not feel like a place where there is treasure. It would feel there might be Mr. Young, old Mr. Young, buried there.

Now it was too late for treasure.

Mr. Lee had begun to burn the house down. He had taken in a bottle of kero and lit a fire with a match.

Smoke was coming out of the roof. Then Mr. Lee came out of the front door. He came down to the gate.

He put the kero bottle in the ute.

"That'll get the old place out of the road," he said.

"There's treasure in there," said Gwenda. "No good now."

"It'll melt," said Morgan. "Now Rick will never see any."

"That's it," said Mr. Lee. "No treasure. The old pirate hid it well away, eh? Deeper than the cabbage patch."

Now a little flame like a flag fluttered at the end of the roof.

Burning wood crackled inside the house.

"It's a good thing he's dead," said Gwenda.

"He isn't," said Mr. Lee. "He's coming to stop with us while he rebuilds."

"I heard him when I went in," said Sophia. "I heard him sneeze out in the backyard. He was in the dunny. I wondered what it was. I thought he might get after me."

"He can't be," said Mr. Lee. "The nong."

But he was. Sophia was right. There was a shout from the burning house. Mr. Lee ran up the side of the house and right through the side fence into the backyard.

When he came back he had old Mr. Young with him. Old Mr. Young was very angry at being left to burn. But he would not sit in the cab of the ute and wait. Instead he leaned on the front fence and watched the flames.

"What about the treasure?" said Gwenda.

"We never found it," said Mr. Young. "And I wouldn't tell you if we did, would I?"

"You would," said Sophia. "She can be nice or nasty and they are both terrible."

CHAPTER 7

THE HOUSE THAT JACK BUILT

"WHAT A SIGHT," said Jack. "What a sight. You'd never believe it."

"Well now, Jack," said his wife, Mary, "you know I believe anything you say by now."

"All right," said Jack, crossly, "believe it if you've got to. I saw some smoke, and I thought to myself, hello, here's a fire, so I went down the street and had a look."

"Listen," said Mary, "I know you. You saw a fire engine and followed that, and that's how you got to the fire."

"And when I got there," said Jack, taking no notice, "there were these two . . ."

"You followed the fire engine," said Mary.

"Details, details," said Jack. "That's got nothing to do with it."

"It's part of the story, and I want to know," said Mary.

"There's no need to go into it," said Jack. "No need. I know what you're going to say, you know what you're going to say. But you don't know what I'm going to say, so shut up and listen."

"If I'm going to say it I'm going to say it," said Mary. "You can't do anything about that."

"Say it," said Jack. "Let me get on with it."

"First," said Mary, "you don't want to be following fire engines; you want an ambulance following you. And second, what did you do to the car?"

"Nothing," said Jack. "There were these two old . . ."

"Nothing?" said Mary.

"Right," said Jack. "These two old . . ."

"What did you do to the car?" said Mary. "Nothing?"

"Nothing much," said Jack. "Little scratch, don't worry about it, I'll fix it. Nothing to it."

"What did you run into?" said Mary.

"Listen," said Jack, "nothing. I didn't run into anything. Like I was telling you, there were these two old boys . . ."

"Don't you go blaming somebody else," said Mary.

"I'm being very patient," said Jack. "I've got a feeling *you* might be running into something in a minute, like a bit of strife. Sit and listen, will you."

"You haven't told me any of the things I want to know," said Mary.

"I haven't told you anything," said Jack. "You keep telling me, and you don't know the story."

"I know some of it," said Mary. "Well, go on."

"Thank you," said Jack. "There were these two old boys leaning on the fence, not a worry in the world, watching their house burn down. I couldn't believe it. I thought I must be seeing things, standing there like that watching it go up, never bothering a bit."

"You went and helped them look, I know," said Mary. "You would like that."

"I was all set to," said Jack. "But if you let me tell things my way you'd know better what goes on. It was just then the fire engine ran in the back of me, and that's what did the damage."

"Damage?" said Mary. "A bit more than nothing?"

"Bit more," said Jack. "That was a way of speaking."

"Could be a bit more than a scrape?" said Mary.

"Bit of a dent," said Jack. "You wouldn't notice it, really, unless you were looking for it."

"Then that's all right," said Mary.

"Yes, well, I'll go on," said Jack. "About these two old . . ."

"Tell me about something else first," said Mary. "I didn't quite understand one thing."

"Just two old fellows leaning on a fence," said Jack.

"Not that," said Mary. "I can't understand something else. If you were following the fire engine . . ."

"I was," said Jack. "I admitted that."

"Following it, right?" said Mary.

"Well," said Jack. "O.K., following it."

"If you're following it," said Mary, "you must be behind it. So how come you get it running into the back of the car, if it's in front of you?"

"Look, let's not be fussy," said Jack. "I could see where it was going, towards this smoke, you couldn't miss it, going up like a house on fire."

"I thought it was a house on fire," said Mary.

"So it was," said Jack. "So you couldn't miss it. So I didn't miss it."

"And you followed the fire engine down and it ran up the back of you. Have I got it right?" said Mary.

"Of course you haven't," Jack bellowed. "I told you, I saw where the engine was going, so I took a shortcut, I got there first."

"What for?" said Mary.

"I know my way about town," said Jack. "I was here before most of it was built. But I wasn't here before those two old boys, I can tell you."

"You're always telling me something or other," said Mary. "Why did you have to get there first?"

"It's obvious, isn't it?" said Jack. "I wanted to find a place to park, so I could see what was going on. That's all."

"You were right in the action, then," said Mary.

"But I haven't begun the story yet," said Jack. "You're just talking about me, and I want to talk about them."

"I'm not interested in them," said Mary. "They're not driving our car."

"Well, if we've settled all that," said Jack, "I'll go on, let them have their turn, fair go."

"Fair go, then," said Mary.

"Fair go on two old fellows leaning on the fence watching their house burn down."

"And forget about you backing the car up against the fire engine," said Mary.

"Now wait a minute," said Jack. "You've been here before. Someone's told you already. How did you know that?"

"I know how to believe you, Jack," said Mary. "I've had a lot of practice."

"I just backed up in the space behind this ute, and, whammo, there's the fire engine."

"Just making this little scratch," said Mary. "Whammo?"

"This little scrape," said Jack. "Little whammo."

"This dent you mentioned," said Mary. "Was that it?"

"Just a little hole, you know," said Jack. "Soon fix it, no worries."

"Whammo," said Mary.

"You keep finding out things I never said," said Jack. "I suppose you think you can tell me about the two old boys. Because I haven't managed to tell you anything about them yet. I suppose you know about them already."

"Leaning on the gate watching the bullocks," said Mary.

"There aren't any bullocks in Iramoo," said Jack. Shouted.

"Just a guess," said Mary. "You leave such a lot out of your stories, Jack."

"I don't believe you listen," said Jack. "Only to the bits I leave out. There's these old boys leaning on the fence, right? And there aren't any bullocks. Just this house on fire. Flames coming up out of the top, smoke going up like I don't know what."

"Like a chimney, perhaps," said Mary.

"Look, I'm telling this story," said Jack. "I'll use my words. Like I don't know what, that's what I said, and that's what it was like. And one old boy says something to the other, and the other says something back. You can tell they aren't in a panic."

"What did they say?" said Mary. "You leave the best bits out."

"I don't know what they said," said Jack. "I was in the car. Just watching. Two old boys, don't speak that loud. And the firemen saying this and that and banging."

"You don't know what they said," said Mary. "You could have got out of the car and heard it all. Couldn't you?"

"I'm just telling you they weren't fussed by the fire," said Jack. "That's what the story's about."

"Foreign, were they?" said Mary. "You didn't know the words."

"I never heard the words," said Jack. "What's the matter?"

"It isn't like you, Jack," said Mary. "You should have been out there leaning on the fence with the bullocks."

"Look, I'm not going to talk to you," said Jack.

"Don't hold out hopes," said Mary. "What were you doing in the car all this time? You could have burned three houses and barbecued the bullock."

"Sitting there," said Jack. "I don't want to get in the way. Just telling you about these two old boys, all calm and peaceful, like it was the sun going down they were watching."

"And you sat in the car watching them watching," said Mary.

"I was talking to the firemen too," said Jack. "A bit. On and off."

"On and off what?" said Mary. "What are you trying to tell me, Jack?"

"Oh well, I couldn't get out straight off," said Jack. "There was the fire hydrant one side so I couldn't open the door, and I'm a bit broad across to get out of the window."

"You never tried," said Mary.

"I did," said Jack. "They had the hose on the hydrant and I got a bit of water in the car. A few drops. But I saw these old boys, I tell you, and laugh; well, I would have; anyone would, just turn and look at the fire engine and take no notice, not a blind bit, you wouldn't think there was a fire."

"You thought there was a fire," said Mary. "Why can't you get out of your side of the car, Jack?"

"Door stuck," said Jack. "That little scratch sort of, you know, pushed the metal along, just buckled it a bit, soon fix that, no problem."

"No worries, I'd say," said Mary. "Just a new side to the car.

"Oh, no," said Jack. "No, no. A couple of new doors, that's all, cheaper than getting them mended."

"And a few drops of water in the other side," said Mary.

"More like a shower," said Jack. "And a bit of paint, touch it up, the duco, where the hydrant touched it."

"Nothing to worry about," said Mary. "Worst bit will be ten dollars for parking against the hydrant."

"No worries," said Jack.

"Nothing," said Mary.

"Nothing much," said Jack.

"Just a new car," said Mary. "That's about it, isn't it?"

"Well," said Jack, "it's just a car. You don't have to have feelings for it."

"I was wrong," said Mary. "You don't need just an ambulance following you; you need a tow truck and a motorcar showroom, to keep you moving."

"Now," said Jack, offended, "don't throw potatoes at me. Think of those two old boys, house burning down, just took it calmly, not a worry in the world."

Mary said something Jack didn't want to hear.

Just walked away calmly. At full speed.

CHAPTER 8

THE TERRIBLE MOTHER

ELISSA WENT ALONG River Street. She was thinking such black thoughts about concrete and tar and trees in straight lines. She was thinking such dark things about how people were unkind to each other and unkind to the world. She was so glad to stop having those thoughts.

She stopped having them when she saw Sophia further along, on the nature strip. Sophia had some dolls and other things with her.

"Sophia is being kind to her dolls and to other things,"

Elissa said to herself. She was glad that people were good, and glad that her sister, Sophia, was one of those people.

Then she smelled the burning wood and paint. Near where Sophia was playing there was a heap of fire. Old Mr. Young had burned his house down. Elissa was unhappy about that, in case Mr. Young had not really meant to have it burned down, though he said he meant it to go. She was unhappy about being so cruel to a house by burning it. Houses should just wear out. Or be handed down to people they fit, like Elissa's shoes.

"People are unkind to houses and land and the sky, filling it with smoke," said Elissa.

She had come to look at the fire. Really, she liked to have sad thoughts. They are bigger than glad thoughts. For her one burned house was the same as a whole city on fire.

Mr. Young was leaning on his front fence looking at the fire. It had been lit the day before and now it was just a large bonfire in the middle of a garden.

The garden all around it was scorched and ashy. How horrible, thought Elissa. How horrible.

"Going well," said Mr. Young.

Elissa thought, Poor man, losing his house. And she thought, How terrible to like burning houses up. So she did not know what to say.

Mr. Young opened the gate and went into the garden.

Elissa thought he thought he was going home. But he only went to poke at the ashes with a stick. Then he came back.

Toddling back, thought Elissa. Mr. Young leaned on the fence again.

"Gwenda's coming," said Sophia. "Listen." Elissa did not need to listen. She could see Gwenda.

It was a bit of a surprise to see Gwenda pushing a doll's pram. That wasn't like Gwenda. Elissa said so.

"That's not hers," said Sophia. "That's ours."

"Yours," said Elissa. "I am never going near a pram again in my life. There are far too many people about already, and babies only add to the number."

However, what Gwenda was doing with it was something to think about, neither sad nor glad. But of course it had to be careful thinking, because if Gwenda found your thoughts were disagreeable to her there was strife.

"It's got her thing in it," said Sophia. "She had it at school one day, and it smelled, and she had it at home and her dad won't let her keep it because of the smell."

"It'll be great for the pram," said Elissa. "Why did you lend it to her?"

"Oh well, she kind of took it," said Sophia. "That's why my dollies are here on the nature strip."

"Oh," said Elissa. Then she thought that perhaps Gwenda had a small relation in the pram, because something was in there sitting up.

"I had to sort of let her," said Sophia.

So they waited for Gwenda, and the pram, and the thing sitting up in it.

It was old Mr. Young who saw that the thing in the pram was not a small relation but a lump of wood.

"You aren't bringing rubbishes to burn on my fire," he said.

"Too right," said Gwenda. "No way. You don't know rubbish when you see it, that's what. This is mine."

Mr. Young leaned over to look at the piece of wood. Sophia had already seen it, and Elissa stayed clear in case Gwenda turned on her. And hurt her as well as making her sad at the thought of unkindness.

But she could see without going close what it was. It was something like the head of a monster.

"Head of a dinosaur," said Gwenda.

"Well, well," said Mr. Young. "Where did you find her?"

"Not her, him," said Gwenda. "It's an it. It was in the river, swimming up and down."

"It was the head of a dragon, a she dragon," said Mr. Young. "Painted red. It was on my boat the night of the flood when it got sunk. My father's boat, when I was little boy. When I still had pigtail."

"Yeah, well, it's mine now," said Gwenda. "O.K.?"

"O.K. fine," said Mr. Young. "I go to Mr. Lee's place now. You stay off fire. Bad for children."

Then he went through his gateway once more, but only to get his stick and stir the fire. He walked off with it.

"I'll help you take it out of the pram," said Sophia.

"What for?" said Gwenda. "I want it in. My dad won't have it round the place no more, so you'll have to take it home tonight."

"Oh," said Sophia, looking at Gwenda, at her dolls and things, and at Elissa.

"You needn't cry," said Gwenda. Then she said, kindly, "You can cry if you like. I don't mind."

"My dolls want to be in there," said Sophia. She was crying a lot now, and tears ran down her cheeks and splashed on the pavement, and more tears and runniness ran from her nose and got licked off into her mouth.

"Oh, come on," said Gwenda. "I haven't done anything to you yet."

Elissa said nothing just then. She was feeling sorry for Gwenda, because she thought Gwenda would be unhappy at making Sophia cry. And she was feeling sorry for Gwenda for feeling sorry when she didn't need to be quite so sorry. It was so easy to make Sophia cry that you couldn't be sorry every time.

Sophia snorted and sniffed, snored up her runny nose and swallowed and began to smile.

Ten years old, Elissa thought to herself. And look at her and listen. Then she thought she was being unkind. Just a little girl, she thought instead.

"We'll have fun instead," said Gwenda. "He's gone away, so we'll go and sit by his fire. You and me and your dollies and things and my dragon. Shall we? Eh?"

"Yes," said Sophia. She had to. Gwenda sounded quite kind, but that didn't mean a thing. Sophia knew it couldn't be true if Gwenda was nice. She couldn't save your life without killing you first.

"Open the gate," said Gwenda. She went through first, with the pram. She did not allow Sophia to put any of her things in it. Sophia was not sure she wanted to, because the head of the dragon or dinosaur smelled so bad.

Elissa leaned on the fence. She was happy looking through the scorched garden at the soil below. That is the real world, she thought. And the ashes will turn to soil and people will be buried in it and the trees will grow up crooked all over the roads. And she stood there thinking about that.

Sophia was crying again.

Gwenda was not doing anything to her. No torture or stones being thrown or ash being put in her mouth. Sophia was standing close to the fire and she had in her hands a doll called Olga, named after her grandmother.

She was crying so sadly. It was nothing Gwenda had done to her. Elissa thought that at first. Then she knew that if Gwenda was there Gwenda must have a lot to do with it.

Sophia looked round. She was sad, sobbing sad, and happy, smiling happy. Elissa knew how she felt. She must be enjoying sadness about something, just as Elissa would enjoy it. And they were sisters, so it was not strange.

Then she threw the doll called Olga into the middle of Mr. Young's fire, the remains of his house.

Gwenda handed her the small painted chest of drawers that Sophia kept leaves in. Sophia took it. She was going to throw that in next.

Elissa thought, Well, she is like me after all. I am glad she is my sister, and I love her for it, but at the same time being me is a very sad thing to be. So she is only a copy, really, and she is being real at the same time. I am so glad she is enjoying the funeral of all her things and dolls.

Then Elissa thought, No, that is a foolish thought. I must not let her burn all she has. That would be murder.

So she opened the gate, ran down the path, and took the chest of drawers out of Sophia's hands. The chest of drawers was very small, of course, and stood in a doll's house.

"Well," said Gwenda, "why don't you go away? She's got too much to carry, and she likes her work. You should leave her alone."

"I guessed it was you," said Elisa. "I think you are a very nasty little girl." And then, feeling horrible at being so unkind, Elissa put her hand in Gwenda's hair and pulled it so that Gwenda had to stand up.

"You're not hurting," said Gwenda. But her eyes had gone large and shiny and soft.

"Good," said Elissa, because it was so painful to be unkind. She let go.

Gwenda laughed.

Every now and then Elissa would lose her temper. She lost it now. She decided that the best thing for the world would be if Gwenda got thrown in the fire. So she tried to do it. Gwenda knew just in time and ran away down among the singed flowers. Elissa got at the next best thing, the head in the pram.

She was very strong then. She picked it up and threw it at the fire. It rolled down out of her hands and into the ashes and red coals and steam began to come from it.

"No," said Gwenda. "No," and she ran into the fire after it, and then ran out again. Now it was Gwenda's turn to be crying and upset. Tears began to come down her cheeks, and they showed because she was dusty from the fire.

Elissa felt the worst she had ever felt in her life. Fancy being unkind enough to make Gwenda feel upset! Her temper went away at once.

"Don't cry," she said. "We'll both go for it," and tears began to run on her face.

No one knows how the next bit went, because of the tears in all their eyes. But it ended with the head in the pram again, a cloud of ashes in the air, a burn on the knee of Elissa's jeans, all the dolls left living put in the pram, and everyone walking down to Gwenda's house together, while Sophia thought how glad she could be, Elissa thought how sad, and Gwenda how bad.

CHAPTER 9

THE DRAGON RUN

MEL WAS AT Joe's house after tea one night. Joe's mother was in, but his father and one grandfather had gone out to the pub for an hour. The other grandfather, the father of Joe's mother, was there.

Mel thought he was a strange old man. Old Mr. Young. He lived in the house, Joe said, but he did not seem to belong to it. He was always getting up and looking at things and asking what they were.

Mel wondered if he had grown too old. He seemed too old to sit still, too old to rest. Joe and his mother were kind to him, all the same, and kept offering him things he might need. "He lives here," said Joe. "We look after him."

So it was a surprise to Mel, what happened. Mel said he had to go, or he would catch it a bit from being late last week.

"Don't want to be late," he said. "They don't care, but it takes them a long time to say it."

"See you, then," said Joe.

Old Mr. Young stood up again. He had stood up a lot during the evening. "I have to go too," he said.

"No, it's all right. You stay here," said Joe, taking the old man's arm and leading him back to the chair.

"Time I went out," said Mr. Young. "I go home."

Then there was a bit Mel did not know about, with Mrs. Lee and Joe and Mr. Young talking in Chinese. During it Mel got to the door.

"Wait a minute," said Joe. "Come with us. I've got to go along with him. Listen," he said in a whisper, "he only came to live with us today and he's forgotten. He thinks it's a long time ago, or something. Mum says to walk him round a bit and get him back."

"I'll come with you," said Mel. "It's not that late yet."

They went out together. It was a warm night. The trams down the end of the road had their doors open. Their wire flashed at the joints as the conductor rod went past.

"Firecrackers," said Mr. Young. "They are leading

the dragons past. I saw the head of a dragon today. It came up out of the river, from my father's boat, and the children were playing with it. The foreign children."

"Listen, Mel," said Joe, "he's just got old and he doesn't know what he's saying. It's all nonsense."

But Mel thought it was not all nonsense. "Kev and I saw it in the river," he said. "But this kid took it off us. She was wild, we couldn't do anything. Then Morgan, you know my brother that gets these ideas, well, he said she took it to school, she's in his grade."

"Well," said Joe, "then he isn't all that mad, is he?" He took his grandfather by the arm and said, "Mel knows about the dragon's head."

"Don't speak about it," said Mr. Young. "He's a foreigner."

Joe turned to Mel. "You can't get through," he said. "He gets like this, everybody isn't Chinese is foreign devils. He's old."

"Good living from foreign devils," said Mr. Young. "I show you the trade. Our boat is the dragon, we do the dragon run."

"Listen," said Joe, "we're taking you home, Grandpa. Home."

"Where does he live?" said Mel. At the moment they were going slowly towards the river.

"River Street," said Joe. "But we've demolished the house. We're going to put another one there and sell it. But he's forgotten, that's all."

"I haven't forgotten," said Mr. Young. "We go down to the river and I show you the trade. The cart is down there. I show you the dragon run. Cheng Li, he show you the track of the snake, and Kai Thaw the path of the rat. But we do the dragon run."

"Listen, Grandpa," said Joe, "that's all been forgotten, they don't do it like that anymore."

"No man forgets the trade he learned," said Mr. Young.

"But they just don't do it anymore," said Joe.

"Tonight I have eaten silver beet, cabbage, onions," said Mr. Young. "Somebody grows them. We go down and see whether the boat comes with them yet."

"O.K.," said Joe.

They walked towards the river.

"It's all right if he's on with the market gardening," said Joe. "But the other part of the story I'm always hearing."

"What part?" said Mel, because he had not heard much yet. Talking about dragons and silver beet wasn't doing much for him.

"You must know," said Joe. "All these old people I meet, seem to think I'm up to the knees in it every night."

"Well, I don't know about it," said Mel. "I saw the dragon, that's all."

They came down to the river. They were at a little wharf, but there was no boat. There was nothing but the water with the streetlamps the other side shining down on the soft slow ripples.

"Not here," said Mr. Young.

"Not been here for about a hundred years," said Joe. "Let's get home, eh."

"We go to the market and find the cart," said Mr. Young. "We can't begin dragon run without the cart."

"We could just go home," said Joe. "Home."

"Foreign people cannot read what we write," said Mr. Young. "So at the corner of the street we mark the sign of the dragon, and Cheng Li the sign of the snake, and Kai Thaw the sign of the rat. But there is much fighting about it. We do our fighting in the gardens. Nobody, no foreigns, ever come to our gardens."

"We can't go to the gardens now," said Joe. "It's too dark to see anything."

"Boat not here," said Mr. Young. "Gardens many way up the river. We bring vegetables every day. Now we go to market and find cart and start our work."

"Look," said Joe to Mel, "he doesn't usually get like this. But my other grandpa knocked his house down this morning and burned the rubbish, and they spent the day leaning on the fence watching it burn, and the sun's got at him, or the smoke, and he's wandering. So don't take any notice of all these rats and dragons. It never happened."

"It's all right," said Mel, "I haven't heard it yet."

"We made much money," said Mr. Young. "Great

money. But we lost the boat. It was all in the boat, and we lost it."

"That's better," said Joe. "That's true. You sailed into the ferry, didn't you?"

"Once we sail in the ferry and knock passenger off," said Mr. Young. "Fancy foreign lady land in the boat. All in the stuff. But not then we lose the boat. Boat sink in big flood, all gone, nothing left."

"We'll go on home," said Joe, "and you can tell us about it."

Mr. Young shook his head. "We go home when the dragon run finish. Or Cheng Li do it and change sign, and big fight in the gardens over load. He take cargo, he take ground and all trade."

"You wouldn't think they'd fight over cabbages," said Mel.

"It isn't just that," said Joe. "I think you're going to get to hear, Mel. But if you talk about it you'll be in strife with me. It doesn't sound right to me, what they used to do, and I'm going to forget it. Come on, Grandpa, we'll go to the market, and then you can go home."

"I show you markings and signs," said Mr. Young. "The dragon run."

"We'll see them," said Joe. "Won't we, Mel?"

"Yes," said Mel. "But we shan't say a word."

"You just pretend you've seen what he shows you," said Joe. "Or he might be around all night."

"I'll pretend all right," said Mel. "If I'm out all night I'll be in too much strife. My dad can get nasty if I go too far. So I'll see whatever he sees."

They walked away from the river, and across River Street.

"We're getting closer to his house," said Joe. "We'll see what happens next, when he gets down to it."

Halfway down the block there was a little alley going down behind the houses. Mr. Young stopped there.

"I show you," he said. "Then when you get the cart you know where to go and what to do. First you see the mark on the corner of the fence. Or on the wall. Or on the ground. It is dark for my eyes. What is the sign?"

"I've got to get it right," said Joe. "He knows them all. I think it's the rat," he said, when he had looked, or acted out a looking.

"No," said Mr. Young, loudly. "There will be fighting if there is a rat."

"Oh, sorry," said Joe. "It's been crossed out. It's the dragon here, no worries."

"Good," said Mr. Young. "We go down here. We can see in the dark. Our noses see for us."

"I don't know what we are doing," said Mel. "I have no idea."

"I know what it is," said Joe. "But I've never had to do it before. In fact I don't think you can do it these days."

"What?" said Mel.

"Come on," said Joe. "He's begun."

Mr. Young had walked down to the back gate that came from a yard into the garden. He seemed to be wanting to go through the fence, but not at the gate.

"The trapdoor is locked up," he said. "The house is empty."

"Trapdoor?" said Mel.

"Well at least there was one," said Joe. "But the next house hasn't got a wooden fence, just corrugated iron. What'll he do now?"

"I don't know what he's doing at all," said Mel.

"He's getting away from us," said Joe. So they went along the alley in the dark and caught up with him.

"It is all wrong," said Mr. Young. "It is the town council. They are driving us away. They do not like Chinamen. Next they will say our vegetables are poisoning the foreigners, and they will close the gardens."

"Never mind," said Joe. "We'll find some other way of living."

"But this is my dragon run," said Mr. Young. "And I will not let Cheng Li have it. This is a trick of his."

"I can't do much with him," said Joe. "Maybe we got in the wrong alley," he said to Mr. Young. "Maybe we'll do better in the next one. Maybe they haven't got the houses up yet."

"Look," said Mel, "he's gone mad, my dad will go wild, and I don't know what's happening either."

"Oh, simple," said Joe. "There's all these outside

toilets across the yard, and they don't have running water, so someone has to empty them, because there isn't a drain, and all these dragon runs and rat runs and snakes are how Grandpa and the others went round, collected the muck from the pots in the toilets."

"Why?" said Mel. "Were they slaves, or something, doing a job like that?"

"No, no way," said Joe. "They got paid for it, going round to get the money each week, so he got the money from the dragon run, and my dad's dad, the other grandpa, got it from the rats, and it all got under one ownership in the end. They took all the muck away in the boat, the dragon was on the front of it. They took it up to the market gardens and dug it in the ground and grew vegetables on it, same as they do in China, and then they sold the vegetables back to the people on the different runs."

"I heard he was a pirate," said Mel. "Treasure and stuff."

"He was," said Joe. "You should hear him and the other one sometimes. But they lost the boat with all the stuff in it, so there's nothing left. But listen, we've got to get him home."

Mr. Young has gone all the way down the alley now, with Joe and Mel following. He was in the street the far side.

"I'll go home now," he said. "It's late. I go just round the corner."

"River Street," said Joe. "I bet my dad's come round there by now, and his dad too."

Joe was right. When they came up River Street there was a ute outside one of the houses, and Joe's father leaning on the cab. Mr. Young looked at him, and then went in at a gate. In a moment he came out. "Going well," he said. "Burning nicely. Just came out to look, with Joe."

Then he climbed into the cab, and Joe after him, and they drove off. Mel walked home alone, thinking about dragon, rat, and snake.

CHAPTER 10

LILLYPILLY

ONE DAY Gwenda began to find something had gone wrong with Sophia, Morgan, Kate, and Darren.

"I mean," she said, "where are they? They've got away."

A whole day went by with no friends for her to hurt. It was not fair.

They were ganging up on her. That was unkind. Gwenda thought it was unkind.

She knew it was unkind, when she thought some more. She would have to find them and keep them in order.

She found a pocketful of stones and got them ready. She knew she would have to hit them into loving her. But she had to find them first.

She had to find them carefully and quietly. Then, she thought, she would know what to do next.

"I might not throw stones," she said. "Just pushing them around might do."

Her mother said, "Why you stay indoors all day? You go play with friends, stop driving me up wall."

Gwenda went out and prowled round the streets. She saw Kate. Kate was shopping with her mother. Gwenda followed quite close. Kate went home, in at the gate, and stayed in. She looked from a window once and that was all.

Gwenda went away. She was cross now. She had not been careful enough. The next person would not see her.

She practiced following people. One old lady she was following turned round and hit her with a newspaper. A man carrying some beer stopped suddenly when she was following him and she walked into his back.

She followed from further away. But then she could not look where she was going and trampled on two tiny children and got shouted at by their mother. Then she walked into a stack of boxes holding tomatoes and scattered them down the street. So she had to run away. And she had forgotten who she was following just then.

Then she saw Darren. He seemed to be following her.

She went away from him. She hoped no one would think she was afraid or running away, or anything like that. She wanted him to go past. Then she would follow him.

He went past. She followed. It was still hard work. She fell over the chains of a shop awning. She banged her ankle on a curbstone. She had a supermarket trolley run over both feet.

But she went on following. They went away from the shops. She had to keep going into driveways. She got stabbed by a sharp pointed plant. She had a sprinkler turned on her when she was under it. A dog bit her on the ankle.

Darren walked along the pavement and none of these things happened to him.

Then Morgan was with him. It was just as easy to follow two people. They never looked round.

Gwenda was following so well now that she wished they would hurry along a bit more. She stood in a gateway and waited while they stood and talked. She looked away for a moment, and when she looked again they had gone.

She knew that Morgan sometimes had ideas about strange things happening to people, but they never came out alive. So that wasn't it.

"If they've followed me instead of me following them I shall kill them," said Gwenda. And she ran down the street to where they had been standing. She got out a stone each for them, and warmed them ready with her hand.

They had gone down a long alley at the back of the houses. They had not had time to go right along it, but they were not there. They had gone.

She thought they must have gone in at one of the gates down one side, into someone's backyard.

She was about to go quietly along and listen and peer through cracks. But then she saw Sophia and Kate coming up the alley from the other end.

So what she had to do was simple. Just watch and see where they went. Keeping out of sight until she knew where it was.

She stayed still.

"Either I'll find out where they're going, or I'll be ready when they get close," she said. She still had two warm stones ready for Darren and Morgan, and they would do for Sophia and Kate.

Of course you have to blink now and then. And in a blink Sophia and Kate vanished. One look they were there, there was a blink and the next look they had gone.

Gwenda waited for a while. They had quite gone. But she knew where they had been. She went down the alley, listening.

She could hear them after a few meters. She heard them talking to each other.

They were not easy to find. They should have been.

One side of the alley was all fence with no doors. The other side had all the doors. She listened at each one. But there was no sound from inside, though she could still hear the talking.

Then she found she had gone past where they were. There was another sound. It was not a talking sound. It was the rustling of leaves and the rattling of twigs.

Gwenda had been thinking of doors and yards. She had not seen the biggest thing in the alley. It had been there all the time. It was a large lillypilly tree, growing on the side with all fence and no doors.

All four of her friends had gone up into it and were climbing about like monkeys and calling like birds. And they did not know she was there.

Gwenda dropped her two stones. She touched the trunk of the tree. She rubbed her nose, because something about the lillypilly tree made it want to run. It made her eyes want to water as well.

It wasn't hayfever. Or tree fever. It was something a lot simpler. Something that made Gwenda turn round and walk home.

It was not the thought of bugs, or spiders. It was something simpler, something about Gwenda herself.

She did not dare climb a tree. She was too frightened of getting up high. She had never been up on the high equipment in the schoolyard. No one had noticed that, but it was true.

If anyone had noticed she would have killed them.

But now she could not get up in a tree with her friends. And her friends did not want her.

So she turned round and went home.

At home she was dreadful. She knew she was. She was in the world's worst temper. She growled at her mother. She threw stones at the cups in the kitchen and broke one. She trod on a cushion until it died all over the floor. Then she had a big fight with her mother and they both screamed. Her mother went out of the front door, Gwenda went out at the back and over the fence and no one had any lunch.

She went back to the lillypilly tree. She was really mad. She was going to stand at the bottom of it and do something really friendly to each of the others as they came down.

There was no one at the tree when she got there. There was not a voice or a rustle. All she heard was the traffic in the distance and the trains in the railway sidings.

She was still mad, though. She took hold of the tree. She thought it might come up in her hands, she was so strong.

But she was mad angry, not mad crazy, and she knew nothing like that would happen.

Of course she pulled and pulled. Something did happen. She pulled herself up into the lowest part of the tree, and stood on a branch.

It was all right. It was sheltered. It was not open like the equipment. The branches and leaves all round held the open sky away from her.

"It's O.K.," she said.

Then she was a little bit higher. She was higher up the tree, but not really further from the ground. And there was another place to hold, and another place to put a foot; and the ground really did not matter. The tree was enough for now.

So she went up, and up and up.

But all at once the sky broke in on her. She had put her head out at the top. All the same, she did not feel high up or afraid. It was like looking out from a big green bed.

She could see into the yards of all the houses. She could see down behind the fence with no doors. It was a creek, or something like that. There were more houses beyond it.

She could not see the alley very well. But she heard people walking in it. They stopped at the tree. They spoke to each other.

The tree began to shake. Someone was climbing it. Gwenda brought her head in and looked down. Darren and Morgan were on their way up.

Gwenda was pleased. She was glad she had found her way into their secret place. She was glad she had found her friends. She was even glad she had used up all her stones at home and had nothing left to throw.

Darren looked up. "Hi, Kate," he said.

"It's me," said Gwenda.

"Get out of our tree," said Darren. He was not at all glad to find out who she was. He must like Kate better, thought Gwenda. She thought that was wrong.

Darren climbed down the tree again. You would think he didn't want to go near Gwenda. Morgan went down as well. In a moment Kate and Sophia came. All four of them stood at the bottom and looked up. And while that was happening Gwenda was trying to come down and join them.

Then they went away without another word, running. And Gwenda took her foot out of the join of two branches, and quickly took the other foot out too, and her hands would not hold her and she fell out of the tree. She slid down a branch and bounced off the end and landed on a slope.

She had fallen over the fence. She thought there was a creek there, but when she had tumbled to the bottom she found it was a rusty railway line.

And she could not climb the fence. It was too high for her. Trees were different. But the tree was the other side of the fence now.

She had to walk along the railway line until it got to a fence. She got under that and she was in the sidings. There she got shouted at again, and she got through the wire to the road.

She went home. She was hungry. Her mother was in. They forgave each other. Gwenda was saving angry for her friends. They had lunch, and then Gwenda had eleven pieces of Band-Aid stuck on her, where she had eleven scrapes. Band-Aid is friendly.

CHAPTER 11

MAD IN THE ARVO

MEL, JOE, AND KEV were walking down from school towards Wilt Street. They found that a boy called Dee was walking with them. At first they thought he happened to be walking the same way and was just the same distance along the road.

They weren't talking about anything private, so it didn't matter. Mel was talking about the footy final, and Joe about some sailing the others didn't know about, and Kev was talking about a motor race.

Dee did not know what they were talking about. He was listening and smiling and looking at each of them in turn.

He stayed with them, even when they stopped politely to give him a chance to move on. He stopped too.

He was younger than them. They did not know him well. He had just been the other end of the classroom all the year, and now here he was, joining them.

"You want something, mate?" said Mel.

"Oh, no," said Dee. Most of all he didn't want to go away.

"Yeah, well the street goes that way and that way," said Kev, pointing up and down it.

"Yes," said the boy. But he didn't go up the street, or down it. He stayed where he was.

"Look," said Joe, "find two other fellows your size. O.K.? You don't want to be with us."

"I do," said Dee. "I've been thinking about it. I've been thinking about it a long time. You're the best ones to be with. Sort of like, you know, I think you're the greatest."

Of course, when someone says something like that you can't get rid of them straightaway. You can't be that unkind. Even if it is only a little sort of kid.

"If we'd wanted you we'd have got a dog instead, anyway," said Kev.

"Nothing personal, he means," said Mel.

"Don't want anyone," said Joe. "Not even you."

So they hadn't said anything unkind. And then they walked away from him. But that was no good, because he walked on with them too.

"I'll be all right," he said.

"I suppose we aren't doing anything," said Mel.

"I'd do anything to join your lot," said Dee.

Mel and Joe and Kev did not know what to do with him. They liked him to think they were worth joining. They thought it was good to be admired. But they did not know what they had done. They did not know why he admired them. And they did not think they were a group of any sort. As far as they knew they met each other quite a lot of times. They did not do anything in particular together. In fact, when Dee came up to them they had been talking about three different things and not listening to each other.

So now they thought they had to be a real gang and get something done to prove it.

But what is there to do going down from school towards Wilt Street? Nothing much, except talk about footy, sailing, or motor racing. And when there were three of them they knew how to walk. When there were four it was awkward. School bags kept hitting the others, and Dee kept getting between and bumping them.

And Dee kept talking. He didn't understand that you can walk down the street without saying anything. Not that he had much to talk about. He only told them how he looked at them all during the term and decided they were the greatest and the most exciting, and he wanted to be one of them.

"You'll have to wait until one of us dies," said Kev. "That way there'll be a vacancy."

"You don't want me," said Dee. "But I'd be all right. I can do things."

"Go on then," said Mel. "Do them."

"Well, there isn't anything just here," said Dee. "I'll do something at the shops. I'll do something at the milk bar."

The milk bar was at the corner of Wilt Street. Mel and the others stopped outside it.

"Go on," said Joe, "do it."

"You've got to come in," said Dee. "I'll shout you. You have what you want."

They all felt insulted then. If the right person wants to shout you then that's great, have what you want. But not little kids from the bottom of the form. Not one of the young ones without any sense.

But of course he wanted to be with them, and that was sense. And there's good tucker in milk bars.

"I'm on a diet," said Mel. The only diet he was on was one of food. But it seemed better than saying no in one word.

"I got this allergy," said Joe. "I get sick from milk bar stuff."

"You keep your money, kid," said Kev.

Then they all looked at each other. They knew what they meant. They knew this kid wasn't for them. They wished they had not refused the shout. If they had said nothing then Dee would have gone into the milk bar and while he was going in they could have run away.

But he might not have understood. But now they all knew they had to lose him. None of them liked to say straight out, Drop dead. It was what they meant but it seemed a bit of a tough thing to say. There was nothing wrong with the kid, but he should choose another lot of small kids.

"Oh well," said Dee. "I've got plenty of money."

"It's the diet," said Mel again. "And Joe has this condition."

"Turns me a different color," said Joe. It wasn't true, though. He was a different color from being Chinese.

Kev said nothing. He was thinking it was like a little sister or something. If you can't get rid of it you've got to make the best of it. He was ready to make the best of it. But he wasn't going to be friendly about it. He didn't owe anything on this kid, and didn't have to send him back the way he came.

"We got to go home," said Mel.

"I'm just coming," said Dee. He closed the wire door of the milk bar and came to them again.

So they went down to Wilt Street and waited at the lights on the corner. A tram came along and stopped.

The lights were green for it, but all traffic behind a tram had to stop when it does.

All four of them crossed part of the way over the road, into the safety zone where passengers wait. There was a chance to cross the whole road now, because the traffic coming the other way had stopped too. Someone was turning right somewhere down the block and the traffic built up behind him, with another tram in it.

That gave Kev a mad idea. He was showing off a bit to Dee, now that he was used to the idea that he was there. He had no time to tell anyone about it.

When they came around the back of the tram their side, he hopped up on the back bar, with his hand on Mel's shoulder, grabbed the rope hanging from the conductor arm, and pulled it.

The arm came off the overhead wire and the tram stopped, Kev pulled the arm down and lifted it under the hook that was there to hold it. There was just time then for them to slip across through the traffic stopped the other side of the road, and get away without being caught.

"You hoon," said Mel. "Run."

They ran. Three of them ran to the pavement. One of them was a bit slower. One of them paused for a moment on the way.

They had gone behind two trams, one their side of the road, and the one coming the other way, ringing its bell at a car on the track.

When they went round the back of it Dee had to prove that he was up to the others in everything. He had seen what Kev did to one tram. He did it to the next.

The conductor arm went up beside the wire. Dee jumped down from the thick bar at the back of the tram.

But the conductor had seen Kev pull his rod down, and was already watching when Dee did the same trick. And when Dee got to the ground there was one conductor in front of him and one behind.

He can stay there for now.

"The dill," said Mel. "Like I said about Collingwood . . ."

"Good though," said Joe. "There's these Mirror classes . . ."

"Ace," said Kev. "Spun off the track and burned up . . ."

Not talking about anything private. Just being together.

CHAPTER 12

A PUFF OF STEAM

MEL, JOE, AND KEV were walking along the alley at the back of a row of houses. It was a Sunday morning and there was not much to do. Mel was talking about a group called The Immortals, Joe was talking about ways of cooking cabbage, and Kev was talking about being a truckie with his own unit, one of these days.

They went up as far as the middle of the alley and passed a big lillypilly tree. When it was behind them Mel said something.

He said, "Go on talking but listen to me and don't turn your heads."

"Are you trying a trick on us?" said Kev.

"No," said Mel. "Listen. You know Dee."

They knew Dee. Dee was a boy who wanted to join them and go with them. But they thought he was useless and did not want him.

"He's up in that tree listening to us," said Mel. "Don't look round. What'll we do?"

"Leave him there," said Kev. "Saw off the bottom of the tree so he can't get down."

But no one understood that. You can't do it.

"Look," said Joe, "we'll have to tell him straight that we don't want him. We'll turn round, walk to the bottom of the tree, climb in it with him and tell him to get lost forever."

So they swung around and marched back to the tree and went up into it as fast as they could.

Dee was sitting in the top. He could tell what they meant to say by the way they looked at him.

"I'm not following you," he said.

"Yeah?" said Kev. "But you're here, aren't you?"

"It's more like you followed me," said Dee.

"Only up in the tree," said Joe. "You know why."

"Look," said Dee. "I kind of took the hint the other day. I'm not following you. I just came up the alley on my way to my grandad's house, and you came up the alley at the other end, so I got up the tree out of the way."

Mel said, "Let's leave him. You can't prove anything with someone like him."

"My uncle lives just over the fence," said Dee. "This is just where he is. It's true what I say. See down there," and he pointed down the other side of the fence of the alley.

"It's a creek or something," said Joe. "We don't believe you, Dee."

"You go down there," said Dee, "and I'll go round to my grandad's house and come through the door and show you what he's got."

"Great," said Mel. "Any of you guys want to see what his grandad's got?"

"No way," said Joe and Kev. "Not him or his grandad, ever."

"Good," said Dee. "I shouldn't have said anything about it."

So that seemed to be all. The three of them climbed down the tree again and went down the alley. Dee climbed down after them and went the other way. They watched him go.

"I wonder what his grandad's got?" said Mel.

"I didn't know there was a creek down there," said Joe.

"We'd better find out about both things," said Kev.

So they went back to the tree and over the fence into a patch of bush. They thought it was the bank of a creek and went down to the bottom. But at the bottom there was a rusty railway line, not a creek. Rusty, with trees beginning to grow up through it. No trains came along here.

If the train isn't coming there's no point in standing by the track. So they walked along it. It went along the cutting and then stopped.

They thought it went against a fence, but when they looked again they saw that the rusty rails ran under a pair of big doors.

"Back of the station," said Mel. "But it can't be. The station's over the other way."

"Tell you what," said Joe, "it's a factory line, there'll be a factory the other side, that's what."

But in a moment or two it seemed unlikely there was a factory beyond, because they heard Dee's voice the other side of the door.

Railway lines. A closed door. Dee's voice. Dee's grandad with something interesting.

"You know what I think," said Mel.

"Yeah," said Kev. "But you're stupid."

"He can't have," said Joe.

But no one was going to stand out and say what they thought was beyond the door.

"One way to find out," said Joe. And he knocked on it with his fist.

"That's them," said Dee's voice the other side. "Grandad, they came, let them in."

"He'll get a surprise if it isn't us," said Joe.

"But it is us," said Kev. "Aren't you?"

There was a rattling of bolts and clicking of keys and the sliding of bars. The doors shook, and then one of them pushed itself open. Or Dee and his grandad pushed it.

There was railway engine beyond the door, in a big shed. It was a steam engine. It was very old and made a long time ago. It was very clean and bright so that it looked new as well.

"It's mine," said Dee's grandad. "It's a Stephenson single-wheeler that used to belong to the State railway, and then was sold to Iramoo Implements Industries, I.I.I. They sold the driver with it, and we retired together and here we are. We sometimes have a run up and down the track here. I was just thinking of firing up and we'll go tonight."

"Oh," said Mel, "what's it like being sold?"

"Like getting married again," said the old man. "It's the only way of keeping the job going."

"He's a bachelor," said Joe.

"He hasn't lived," said the old man. "Now, you want a ride, you bring some coal or those nasty briquettes or we shan't have a blaze. Did you tell your friends that, Dee?"

It was one thing to look at the engine for an hour. That was good and interesting, but didn't last forever. But it was another matter if people were going to think they were Dee's friend. If anything Dee might be their friend, but they were not even going to let that happen.

So they looked, and then Mel thought it was lunch-time, and they went away again without promising any coal or briquettes. Bringing anything like that would make Dee the friend of the group, and they knew that was impossible.

They went home and had lunch. "I can't come out after," said Mel. "My dad and I got some work to do."

"Got to go see my aunty," said Kev.

"That's O.K.," said Joe. "See you tomorrow."

But Mel had decided he would go back with some fuel for the engine and have a ride on it. After lunch he took four of the plastic packs of briquettes and humped them to the alley, under the tree, over the fence, and along the cutting.

He saw that Dee had already been bringing some, because there was a small stack outside the doors.

He was wrong. It was Joe that opened the door.

"It's like this," said Mel. "Well, I thought if I came alone we wouldn't have to have him in with us."

"I thought the same," said Joe. "But let's kill Kev when he comes, telling lies about his aunty."

So they jumped Kev when he came and no one minded that much.

After that there was a lot to be done. Mr. Olanik, Dee's grandad, had them polishing and greasing and carrying water and getting hotter and hotter and more and more dirty themselves. The fire in the engine was lit, but the engine was in the shed so the smoke had nowhere to go, and the heat had no escape. He had them walking down the track as well, cutting down the small trees that had grown up in the last year. The engine had not been out for that time.

The trip, when it came, took about ten minutes, longer than Mr. Olanik meant to take. First there came a moment when he pulled a lever and they heard steam crack its way along a pipe and then stand for a short time without doing anything.

Then there was a sort of a small shake in the engine, and from the wheels there came a noise like sugar being trodden on, which was the rust on the rails being powdered. From the engine itself came a puffing roar and there was movement, and then there was going.

Slowly they went down the length of the cutting, past the lillypilly tree, out to where the cutting opened out and there was a wire fence ahead, with the rails going under it and into the goods yard and the workshops of the State railway.

"This is how far we go," said Mr. Olanik. He stopped the engine and had another tube of beer. He had a pack with him, because he had worked hardest and was hottest.

"We go back now," he said. They slid back into the cover of the cutting.

"Not very far," said Dee.

"Not far enough," said Mr. Olanik. The engine went backwards as far as the lillypilly tree and stopped. "Not far enough," he said again.

And then they were moving forwards again, and this time they did not stop at the end of the cutting but went further.

"No one about Sunday," said Mr. Olanik, and they did not stop at the fence but went through it and they were on the State railway line.

"Well, this is too far now," said Mr. Olanik, peering ahead. "We go one way we crash into a truck. We go the other we come off the rails at the points. We get our best choice and go home again. But first, I show them I'm here."

His way of showing he was here was to blow the whistle of the engine three times, and then put the lever over to reverse and take them back the way they had come. They went through the broken fence, into the cutting, and stopped.

"Look what some foolish person done to the fence," said Mr. Olanik. "Must have been a cow on the line, did you see a cow, charging about?"

"Yeah, big mob," said Kev.

"They don't let me drive on their lines, I send my cows through their fence," said Mr. Olanik. "Now we better go home or they see us."

So they went back, slower and slower, because there

was not much steam left. Then it was tea-time, and their visit was over.

The next few days they expected trouble from Dee. He was bound to be a pest to them. But he was not. He stayed away, not bothering them at all.

"He isn't so bad," said Joe.

"He's just getting at you by being nice," said Kev.

"Don't think about him," said Mel. "He doesn't come anyway near."

But next Sunday it was the three of them that loitered near the lillypilly tree, in case things began to happen anywhere along the cutting.

Nothing happened. In the end they went down to the rails and walked up to the doors. But all was quiet there, and no one answered their tap on the wood.

And at the State railway end of the cutting they found the wire fence up again. And the rails that ran under it were lifted from their bed and laid to one side.

Mr. Olanik had showed the railway something with his whistle. And they had shown him something back. He couldn't easily get out on their roads again.

"Well, poor old guy," said Joe.

"Can't even take his wife out for a drive on Sunday now," said Kev. It wasn't exact sense, but the meaning was clear.

CHAPTER 13

THE LOOK-ALIKE

DEE WAS IN the city with Kate. They had been to see a film about an aircrash. Getting in the place had worked well, following behind a lady with her own child and pretending to belong to her because children under fourteen were not allowed in on their own.

Watching had been a failure because Kate had been rotten right through it, and wouldn't watch the good bits, and wanted to go out.

But you get bugged by your little sister even if she's

doing it all right. You're going to lose out.

So they were waiting for the lights to change and let them across the road for the bus. Dee was thinking about losing Kate before he got home. I mean, he thought, she's a creepy kid, not liking a few bodies and flames and stuff. Because if you leave her alone she collects dead bodies, or bits of them, like hair, and fingernails, and feathers off the bird. Perhaps she's going to be a doctor and collect wee-wee.

Then the lights said walk. "Get on," said Dee, and gave Kate a push, and she went.

Before he could get moving properly someone got his arm. Dee thought, Now what? It was the sort of hold that meant trouble was coming, firm and sudden. Dee knew it from the time he messed with a tram. Now he thought it might be from the theater when they found he and Kate got in alone.

What held his arm was the hand of a girl. She was a year or two older than Dee and not very friendly. But she did not look like trouble with trams or theaters.

As a matter of fact, she loked rather like Kate giving trouble. On one of the days she was right.

"You're not just walking off like that," she said. "You think you can do what you like, but you aren't going to."

Dee would have said something about not knowing what she was talking about or who she was, but he didn't get the chance. She let go of his arm. For a moment he thought that it had all stopped happening and he could go. She must have found out she didn't know him. But it went on.

She had a brown paper parcel under her other arm. She dumped it on him.

"You take this home," she said. "They're yours. I'm not going to fetch and carry for you, and nobody else is either."

Then she put his hands round the parcel, turned round, walked away a pace, and turned and looked and said, "Yes, you take it home."

Then she had slipped away and Dee was looking round for Kate.

He had sent her on, and missed the lights himself. So where was she? Of course he planned to lose her on the way home, but not just here like this, not too really.

And the cross girl with the parcel had been too much like her. But where was Kate?

Kate was in the middle of the street, coming back for him. Looking cross. And from the other side of the crossing there was a tram coming down ringing its bell, and a panel van, and they never look where they are going.

So he'd lost Kate. It was like the pictures, but less exciting and more real.

Kate calmly walked back. The tram stopped for her.

The driver shook his head. The panel van stopped. Kate must have given it the death ray with her eyes.

"You nearly got killed," said Dee, when she had come back to him.

"Oh, no," said Kate, still calm about what she had done. "They stopped." But she was angry about being sent on alone. "It wasn't even thrilling." she said. "I didn't have to close my eyes."

They got across together at the next change. What can go wrong if you obey the lights?

Apart from strange girls giving you strange parcels.

"You went shopping," said Kate, when they were on the bus. "I didn't see you."

"Oh, shut up," said Dee. He had nothing to say about the parcel, nothing in the world. He was going to leave it on the bus, but Kate had seen it and he had to go on carrying it.

He carried it home.

Dee had to wait a bit. Kate was bad enough, but blimey, Mum was the limit. Though he wondered about strange girls at traffic lights. There's all sorts in the city. Maybe it was a pack of scalps for Kate. Or a set of skin. Or teeth. Kate had jars of teeth from people.

She didn't care about fairy money.

"It just got put in my hands," he said. "Some girl did it."

"Perhaps it's a poor unwanted baby," said Mum.

The things they think of, thought Dee. Of course, that's what Kate is saving all the bits for, a person. I'll get her a bolt to go through its neck.

"It feels like clothes," said Dee. "But it's yours. She said to take it home."

"Well, I don't want charity," said Mum. "I'd better look inside. They can have it back."

But she was hoping it was something marvelous she could keep. She hoped her name was inside.

"Ee-yip," she said, when she had it open. "Some shops are too great to put their name outside, but they're not too great to send the bill. Who did she think you are, Dee? One of those people the other side of the city, all the money in the world and everything, take all give nothing. Not that I would take it."

She was talking away. She was talking about what was in the parcel. It was clothes of some sort. Dee bothered to have a look, all that creamy white cloth.

"What is it?" he said. He didn't much want to know about dresses and things.

"I don't know," said Mum. "But look at the price, eighty-five dollars. I can't read the writing on the bill what the eighty-five dollars is for." Then she was taking the things out of the bundle and opening them out.

"Is there anything you didn't tell me?" she said. "You don't get picked for the test or something, Dee, and forget to tell me?"

"You're mad," said Dee. "What way could that happen?"

"But look," said his mum, holding out a pair of white cricket trousers, "just your size and this nice stuff they're made of. What girl is it you get these from?"

"Kerry Packer," said Dee. "No, I don't know anything about it all. I was just standing there when she puts it in my hand and tells me to take it home."

"Well, you take it back," said his mum. "You took it, you take it back," and she folded up the trousers and put them away. "It's all written on the bill, no worries. I can't read it, but you can, you got better eyes, you must have or they wouldn't pick you for this cricket team."

Then the pressure was off him because Kate came in with a cut finger asking what she could keep blood in. Mum was more on about what she could keep it away from, namely this parcel of stuff.

So Dee bundled it up as well as he could. But of course it wouldn't pack down the same. Then he puzzled out the writing on the bill while he waited for his tea. There was a name and address at the top of the print. That was the shop. There was another name and address in writing, and that took some reading. But he got it clear after a bit. It was the other side of the city, and city trams went there.

"Well," said Mum, "you got the words out of it yet?"

"Sure," said Dee. "What's for tea?"

"That doesn't matter much," said Mum. "You take that back where it should be. Where does it come from?"

When Dee had told her the address she gave him the bus fare and something for the tram out the other side of the city. "Now go," she said, "I wouldn't care if you stole it, but this way is stupid. Get it out of the house."

She wouldn't listen about tea. She would not.

Some people would make you cry, thought Dee, as he walked down to the bus. If you went in for that sort of thing.

In the bus he could hardly tell whether it was belly grinding, or the gearbox. Both wanted attention, it could be.

Later on his inside whined and whinged with the motor of the tram. And then, when he had found the suburb he still had to walk to the address, along quiet avenues with great green hedges and full-grown trees on the nature strips. And as he went on, no one about to ask the way from.

But he found the house at last. Carrying the parcel and a dead stomach. Kate could start a collection with it.

When he got to the door he knew what he should have done. He should have left the parcel on the tram and let someone else sort it out and gone home and had tea.

Now he could drop it on the doorstep and walk away.

Apart from dying of hunger in the gutter on the way back, he would be all right.

But the door opened in front of him. It was the right house. There was the girl again.

"What are you doing out here?" she said. "You're in the dining room."

She held the door open and he went in. The smell of food nearly killed him. The dining room was just there, same as the kitchen would be at home, and the table was covered in food. All on plates and dishes and racks and bowls, not a packet in sight.

This was where a parcel of cricket clothes cost eighty-five dollars.

Round the table were people, eating the food. They all turned and looked at him. And one of them was himself, looking back at himself.

"A look-alike," said a man. "This is John. What's your name?"

"Dee," said Dee.

"You just came in time," said the girl. "They were killing me about that parcel."

"And me," said the look-alike. "The dill gave you my clothes."

It was clear what had happened. It didn't make this family forgive each other. Or if they did forgive each other a little they blamed Dee instead.

But first they brought him a chair and filled him a

plate. He spoiled Kate's collection by giving his stomach the kiss of life with a lump of roast lamb and potatoes, pumpkin, parsnip, sweet potato, carrots, and peas. Partway through he thought they had stopped, he could only hear his own knife and fork. But they were eating so daintily they didn't seem to get down to the plate, you'd think they had brushes, not forks.

"I saw him there," said the girl. "It was just like him, going off and leaving me to do it all. So I gave it to him."

"Lucky to get it back," said the man.

And Dee and the look-alike, John, kept their eyes away from each other. You don't like yourself the other side of the table. You don't know who you are.

"You stay here," said the look-alike, at last. "I'll go back to your place. It can't be worse than this."

"No way," said Dee. "Anyway, I'm me; you just look like it."

That was what he felt. There wasn't anything you could do with somebody who just looks like you. So you might as well go home, even if it's just bloody Kate and the packets and wrappings on the table every time. The look-alike is only a copy. Dee is the real one, he thought. Dee, me I'm the proper one.

There was a lot of thank you and so on about, and better than that. The man asked where he lived, and then took him all the way to Iramoo, and there he was, home. And Kate squalling and collecting snot with her finger up her nose, and he never got even an offer of tea.

And of course he had done better, and of course he wondered if somewhere else might be where he would want to live. But not where he would be a copy. Because he knew he was the only real one of him, Dee. And in some ways there isn't anyone else, whatever they look like.

CHAPTER 14

COME OUT TO PLAY

WELL, YOU CAN'T remember everything.

Kate looking for Darren or Gwenda. Sophia looking for anybody but Gwenda.

"I can't come out," said Darren to Kate. "I've got the twins."

"No way can I get out," said Gwenda. "But I don't mind. I've got Ilich for the day. He's my cousin or my uncle or something to baby-sit. Or he might be my aunt. I haven't looked."

"I can't," said Amanda to Sophia. "Look at him, he's called Andrew."

"I know him," said Sophia. She went off to find anyone but Gwenda. She found Darko. He was in the garden at the front of the house.

"I'm looking after Marija," he said. "I don't want to but I have to."

Sophia went to find Darren.

"Where's everybody going?" said Darren. "Gwenda just came round too. I've got the twins today. Why don't you go and find Gwenda."

It wasn't quite a question, so there was no need to answer. But of course Sophia did not want to find Gwenda, who would pull her hair, torture her, and throw stones at her when she ran away.

But she could not help going past Gwenda's house. She saw Gwenda with a baby and wondered whether she was practicing unkindness on it, or training it in armed combat ready to win over all other babies. She looked as if she was just playing with it and making it happy.

Sophia nearly spoke to her, seeing she was in such a good mood. She went away instead and visited.

Just up the street, at the same time, Kate was visiting Con.

Con and Mike had a baby each, Drina and Wendy. But Kate and Sophia met.

"I'm just looking for anybody," said Kate.

"So am I," said Sophia. "But they're all engaged."

"I think they're married, with all these babies about," said Kate.

"I can't find anybody, only you," said Sophia.

"I feel like a lot of people and going to the park and doing something," said Kate.

So they went together to Morgan's house. Morgan had Rick on the end of a rope, as usual.

"He won't do anything I want," said Morgan. "I thought they were getting a dog, but it was just this. And Mel never has to look after him. It's always me. I sometimes think he's imaginary, but he won't go away. I sometimes think he's only a dream, but I don't wake up."

"Leave it," said Kate. "There isn't anyone. We just want to go to the park, but there's not enough of us."

"I'll have to carry him all the way," said Morgan. "He weighs a ton."

That was a start. "We'll get Gwenda," said Kate. "You go and tell her, Sophia."

Sophia was good at doing what she was told. So off she went to Gwenda's house, forgetting what might happen to her.

"We could all go," said Gwenda. "Just write a note for my mum, Sophia."

"I don't know what to say," said Sophia.

"I'll write it," said Gwenda. "You carry my uncle."

So Sophia carried Gwenda's uncle, and they collected

Darren and Darko and Con, and Kate collected Amanda and Mike.

Sophia went on carrying Ilich. Kate carried Rosie, one of Darren's twins, and everybody else carried their own family baby. Gwenda, of course, carried no one.

That's how it usually worked out.

They went to the park. You can get there along the Salt River, going past the tallow factory and its smell, and under the road to the city, and there is the park, along the Salt River where it is cleaner, and there is green grass.

Now it was quite simple. It is just as easy to watch eight babies as it is one. Or two, like Darren. So they started by keeping an eye on them all.

Then it got so that only the people who really liked littlies kept an eye on them.

Then some people seemed to go away from the baby-minders. Morgan and Mike went off to the riverbank and called across to Joe Lee, who was on the other side, but no one knew what he was doing.

Darko and Darren began to play their own game of tracking and trailing and killing each other. They went right to the top end of the park and waited until they heard a train coming and then saw it rumble over the trestle bridge much higher up the river, where it stopped being the Salt River and became the Iramoo.

Morgan and Mike went down the river a bit and crossed on the stock bridge near the tallow works, to see what Joe was doing. They shouted back something about Rick and Wendy, and it was not hard to guess that they would be coming back soon.

Sophia was the one left to guess it.

Darko and Darren shouted and waved from their end of the park. You could tell what they meant.

Sophia was the one that told herself.

Con went off with Amanda. Amanda was trying to get one of the swings over the top. She had Con sitting in the swing. She wasn't going over the top herself. She stayed on the ground and pushed. They kept looking back to Drina and Andrew. In fact they came back once and counted them both, and then off again.

Then they were not at the swings anymore.

Sophia thought they had probably left a message in the air somehow, saying someone had to watch the babies for them.

Sophia was there watching.

"He likes you," said Gwenda to Sophia. But she only meant her baby uncle did. That was another message for Sophia to look after another baby. Gwenda and Kate went away. They just went. They didn't go slowly out of sight like the others. They went out of sight.

Sophia sat with her eight babies.

"They don't belong to me," she said to a blackbird on the grass.

The blackbird seemed to think that eight was not very many. She took away a worm.

A baby cried. Sophia wished she knew their names. She could only be certain about the uncle.

But she did not know what he wanted when he cried.

She did not know what any of them wanted when he cried.

So of course they went on crying.

Then Sophia thought she would go home. The babies could find their own way.

"They have instincts," said Sophia. "They're more like animals."

And she stood up to go. She stood up to leave them. And she could not leave them.

"But they're not so clever as animals," she said. "They won't find their way anywhere. Morgan's right. A dog would be better."

And she longed and longed for eight little puppies instead.

And she sat there and waited. No one came back.

Even kittens would do, thought Sophia. I could pick them up and go home.

Then a rather cross lady came to where she was sitting, sorted through the babies, and took one.

"I think that one belongs to Mike," said Sophia.

"When I want you to tell me which is my own baby," said the cross lady, "then I'll speak first."

Then she went away. She met two more cross ladies on the way out of the park and waved them towards Sophia. They came and took three babies, smacked two of them, and looked as if they were thinking of smacking Sophia.

Sophia sat a little way from the four that were left. She thought she could go home now, but still she couldn't get up and leave them all.

Another lady came and took one. The three that were left went on growling and howling. Sophia went a little further away. But that was too far, and she had to come back.

She sat the babies the right way up. They went on crying.

Another lady came and took the biggest. There were two left now. One was the uncle.

The uncle's mother came, complete with Gwenda's mother.

"You bad girls," said Gwenda's mother. Sophia felt she must have been very naughty.

A little old-looking sort of mum came and took the last baby. Now there were none. Sophia thought she could go home.

But she felt she should wait a bit longer. The babies had gone, but their sisters and brothers might come back to see how they were. Someone had to tell them. And Gwenda, with an uncle gone, might be worse than ever.

Sophia sat and looked at the river. She had wanted a lot of people, children, babies, and mums. Now there was no one left. Never mind.

Then the others all came back at the same time, from different places.

"Where is he?" said Gwenda.

"Where are they?" said Darren.

"You should hold his rope," said Morgan.

"Their mothers took them," said Sophia. "They knew which was which."

"I forgot all about Andrew," said Amanda.

"Well, let's go home," said Gwenda. "You can't remember everything. Not all day long."

But most of them did get some remembering done when they got home. Their mums reminded them.

No one said thank you to Sophia. But she had had a good afternoon. Well, none of the babies, not even Uncle Ilich, had thrown a stone at her.

CHAPTER 15

CITIZEN BAND

KATE SAID SHE had one end of a two-way radio, citizen band stuff.

"I'm collecting voices now," she said. "From people that aren't there anymore."

"You can't speak to the dead," said Dee.

"You can," said Kate. "But it's like speaking to you, nothing happens. It's broken that way."

Dee took no notice of the whole thing. Of course Kate had nothing of the sort, not real. She would have a thing made of wood.

And then again, she had so much stuff like hair from everybody, and toenails, that she might have hit on some witch way of doing things.

"Anyway," said Kate, "it's not dead people. It's only live ones."

"Sure," said Dee.

Kate went into the yard again. Dee switched on his end of the TV system, the bit that talks to you. You can't send messages through that either. It isn't made that way.

Kate came in. "They're going to the river," she said.

"Oh, phooey," said Dee. "Go away, will you. I don't want to hear your stupid ideas. Go and play by yourself."

She went away. Before long Dee found there was nothing to watch. He went into the yard after her.

He was only going to tell her she couldn't hear anything from a C.B. radio made of wood or cardboard boxes. He knew that was what she had, with nailheads for buttons and pencil marks for dials and a bit of stick for an aerial.

But what she had was what she said. He saw her holding the glitter of a real radio to her ear. He heard the real voices coming from it. The antenna shone in the sun. The knobs were real plastic, the dials real glass.

He was angry at being wrong. He was jealous too. He was easily jealous.

"That can't be yours," he said. "Give it to me."

"It isn't yours either," said Kate. And when he came

near she put her foot up his belly, killing him in about six places. Probably collecting real live whole dead people now.

She must have stolen it. She would be collected now, her fingerprints in the police book. Her, locked away in a police prison.

"Con gave it to me," she said. "It's broken. You can't talk to them, I said."

Dee took a breath. He had to. But she had got him just under the ribs as well as everywhere else and it hurt to breathe.

"It's just one of those old ones," he said. "Out of date now. You can only hear one band. The new sets have got twenty-three bands."

"One of them's found the raft," said Kate. "The others are going to join him. He's called Joe. The other ones are Kev and Mel."

"I know them," said Dee. "Friends of mine." Not quite true. They were friends of each other, and he wanted to join them, but so far he had not quite got with them.

There was one time that had been good, but that had been Dee's grandpa's thing, not Dee's.

"And you can't hear all that," he said. "That's just old, old, old. You could get the law on you for having that old thing working."

Kate looked at him and smiled. "Oh phooey," she said. "Go and play by yourself."

"I'll buy it from you," said Dee.

"O.K.," said Kate. "It isn't very interesting now. I don't know all they're saying."

"Let's listen," said Dee. "I'll know."

"It isn't yours. You can't listen," said Kate. "You buy it and then you can. But not before."

The price came out to be a dollar and an eyebrow. The eyebrow was for Kate's collection of bits of people. Dee got the price down to ninety cents in money and ten cents instead of the eyebrow.

"A bargain is a bargain," said Kate, giving him the C.B. set, taking the money, and going out of the yard. "I'm getting my lunch," she said.

The C.B. spoke.

"Anything your *crrrrrr*, Kev?"

"*Crrrrr* up here, but there's *crrrrr crrrrr crrrrr* if you *crrrrr*."

"*Crrrr sn sn sn choop choop* the water."

"Right on, Kev."

"*Choop choop* chestle, Melxchx."

"O.K. *bloop*."

"*Bleep* Joe, *cush cush cush cush crush*. Get under when the rain goes high *sn sn sn cush crrrr choop*."

Trust a girl to wreck a thing like this, thought Dee. You should take care of things like this, even if they are out of date.

But Dee had heard it more clearly than it can be written down.

The first voice was probably Mel, saying, "Anything your side, Kev?" Something to do with Kev being on the bank of the river. Probably the Salt River, Dee thought when he first heard it. But he changed his mind later.

Next was probably Kev's reply. "Nothing up here," but what there was *crrrr crrrr crrr* of, if somebody *crrrr*ed, Dee could not guess.

Then somebody else, probably Joe, wanted something to do with water. Dee thought it might be something under the water, but no one on the C.B. was very excited about it.

Then Mel told Kev he had guessed something right.

Then Kev told Mel something that showed exactly where they were, and what river. The next remark had something to do with the trestle bridge, where the train crossed the Iramoo at the place where it stopped being the Salt River, where the end of the tide was.

So Kev and Mel and Joe were up the Iramoo, near the trestle bridge. That was a good guess. But the next bit of talk proved it.

"Get under when the train goes by," was what it said, if you were listening to yourself listening. Even if it was the oldest C.B. set in the world and badly treated by your sister.

Dee thought about lunch. Then he thought there were other things more important. For instance, now he knew where someone was without seeing them, two kilometers away.

It was like being invited to go to them. They were there calling out and he was the only other person hearing them.

They must know they were calling him. Even if they didn't know what they were doing they would have to agree that they had called.

So lunch could look after itself. And Dee still felt a bit sick from Kate's kick across the belly. But not too sick to take to the streets and go where he had been guided.

He listened all the way. There was a lot of switching on and off, he thought, but no words very much. Except that Kev once, "The Martians have landed, the Martians have landed. Oh no they haven't, it was *crrrrr choop.*"

It has always been *crrrr choop* so far. But Dee did not think about that. He wondered about Kev. People at school wondered about Kev, but he seemed to get by.

Dee went down to the river as soon as he could. He went along the bank and under the road by the tallow factory. The smell made him close his throat. He felt a bit more sick.

Then he crossed the park, all the way along the edge of the Salt River. Then he was at the far end and took to the riverbank again.

He had been able to see the trestle bridge from the

park, a fair way off. Then he lost sight of it round a bend of the river. When he saw it again he was much closer.

The C.B. crackled again. It spoke more clearly.

"We'll come in now," said Mel.

"The water's clear," said Joe.

"Clear?" said Mel. "It's about as clear as a thick shake."

"Clear of shipwrecks," said Joe.

"Why don't we go down on the raft?" said Kev.

"That'd be a shipwreck too then," said Mel. "We'd drown in the thick shake."

"Down to the town instead of walking," said Kev.

"No way," said Mel. "We'd have to pole down and pole up again and it's quicker to walk, because we have to come back here and look at the next bit of river up by the Sanctuary."

"What if we find it's up in the platypuses?" said Joe.

The C.B. went on telling their conversation. Dee did not hear it for the moment, because someone was coming along the path behind him, and he turned to see who it was.

He thought it might be Mel and Joe and Kev, because he had not seen them yet. He did not want to be found by them before he worked out what to tell them about spying on them, bugging them.

The person coming along the path was Kate. She came straight up to him.

"I followed you," she said.

"You shouldn't follow people," said Dee. "That's not right."

"I want it back," said Kate, putting her hands, both of them, on the C.B. set. "I've spent the money and I want it back."

"Fair go," said Dee. "I paid you. It's mine now."

"Is it ever," said Kate. "It's Con's. He wants it back, doesn't he?"

"It's mine," said Dee, and he pulled it away from Kate, and she pulled it away from him. It was in the middle of a speech, too. How very impolite of them.

The C.B. set whirled up into the air, still talking, and landed in the long grass between the path and the river.

It went on talking. Dee and Kate ran for it.

Someone else got there first. Joe had it in his hand. Dee and Kate stopped, and waited.

The C.B. went on speaking. It spoke in Mel's voice.

"I'll just have an order of chips," he was saying. "I'll catch up."

Joe was carrying his own C.B. as well. He spoke into it, and his voice came out of Dee's set too. He told Mel to come right along. Mel came right along. Kev came first, though.

"Where'd you get that oldie?" he said.

Mel said, "Where did you get that, kid?"

"It's mine," said Kate.

"No it isn't," said Dee. Then he thought he should have said it was Kate's and be out of bother with Mel. "Yes I mean no," he said.

"You followed us up with it?" said Mel.

"Yes," said Dee. He thought he had paid a dollar and might as well keep the set.

"We don't like that," said Mel. He took Dee's C.B. and looked at it. "Spying. We don't like it. Don't do it anymore."

"No," said Dee. There was nothing else he could say, but he did not quite mean it.

Mel meant it. He bent his elbow, and threw the set out into the Salt River. "Good-bye to that," he said.

"Good-bye to *crrr* splash," said Dee's C.B. And he wondered whether he would be next.

But something else happened then. Kate was angry at once. She went for Mel with her nails, and the same kick that she had given Dee earlier on. Mel got her by the kicking leg, and held her there.

She screamed at him. She spat, but not very well and got it in her hair. Then she fell down and sobbed. Just like a girl, Dee thought.

Then Joe and Kev were picking her up and listening to her, and were being sorry for her. Because after all it was Con's C.B. and she should never have sold it because it was not hers. And now it was in the river. And Dee had lost his dollar too. And Kate explained it all, you could hear her a mile, you didn't need a C.B.

Mel felt very guilty about throwing it in the water. He came to Dee and gave him a dollar to put that part right. He said he would see what he could do about another old C.B. for Con.

Then Dee felt very strange indeed, because he had done badly and not lost. Suddenly, somehow, the riverbank went shaky in front of his eyes, and there were tears running down his cheeks, and they would not stop.

Then he and Kate were alone. She was happy now, and counting money.

"Seven dollars," she said. "I shall keep it forever."

"You have to *crrrr sn sn sn choop*," said Dee. He tried again. "You have to give it to Con," he said. *Cush cush* said his nose.

"Con?" said Kate. "I'll just say I lost the radio thing. He won't care. His dad has a shop full of them. He can get another any time he wants."

There is nothing you can do about sisters like that but see them home gently.

CHAPTER 16

A MAP OF THE WRONG PLACE

IF PEOPLE CAN'T read your thoughts, and you haven't said anything about it, then how does Sir know what you are going to do?

There were two school excursions on one day. The two top grades were going to one place. The next two grades were going to another.

Kate was in the lower group. They were going to the wildlife sanctuary up the river. But she wanted to go in the other group, who were visiting the city jail.

So she thought about it. She knew that thinking didn't show. She knew that what Gwenda was thinking didn't show. Gwenda offering you a dusty lolly she didn't like looked just the same as Gwenda throwing a stone at you.

So how does Sir know?

Kate got herself ready for the city jail. Not ready for a long stay, just a visit.

She got herself unready for the Sanctuary. She was not interested in animals. She was interested in the hangman's rope that someone had worn.

So she made no arrangements about sitting next to anyone on the way to the Sanctuary. And so no one knew what she was thinking she made no arrangements about sitting next anyone on the way to the city jail.

You could get found out that way.

You get found out anyway.

She got a plan of the city jail. She read it and she read it. She knew the Governor's Quarters. She knew the Warders' Houses. She knew the Outer Courtyard. She knew the Inner Courtyard. She knew the Tower. She knew the Kitchen. She knew the Flogging Room. She knew the East Wing and the West Wing. She knew the Cells. She knew the Gallows. She knew the Chapel. She knew the Gates, both of them. She knew the Outer Wall. She knew the Watch Points. She knew the Iron Gates in the corridor. She knew the Death Cell. She knew the Cemetery.

She could have lived there, she knew it so well. But

she planned a short visit. A short visit with the grades five and six.

Her grade was going to the Sanctuary. Kate did not want to see the wild animals.

She wanted a skeleton. A skeleton with a broken neck. A skeleton still hanging from the gallows.

A skeleton and its ghost.

It was hard to keep it all quiet. She had to play at being excited about the Sanctuary. She had to say, Oh how sweet is the Koala. She did not care about Koalas. She had to say how rare is the Platypus. She did not care about the Platypus, that looked like a worn slipper. She had to be happy about thumping Kangaroos. She thought the Kangaroo could thump and jump off the edge, she didn't care.

So she tried to look as if she cared. She was really thinking about other things, like whether Liza's scab on the graze she got on the swing, whether that scab was ready to come off Liza's knee. And whether she could ask for it for her collection of bits of people.

The jail was more likely to have bits of people. The wild animal sanctuary only had Australian animals, no lions or tigers or elephants that might start eating people and leave a few interesting scraps about.

If only I lived in Africa, Kate thought. The animals are more sensible. I would keep a lion. They feed themselves.

The next best thing here was the jail.

On the day of the excursion Kate began wrong. She forgot she was going to the Sanctuary. She remembered she was not going to the jail.

She got to school without her lunch and without a lunch order.

She was sort of thinking that before they hang you they give you all the breakfast you could want, whatever you like. She was sort of thinking that would do for lunch.

She forgot to take a raincoat of some sort. A jail has a roof on it.

She wasn't thinking. She knew that when she got to school. Sir said she should pair up with Morgan when they walked down to the station.

But Morgan was not going anywhere. Oh yes, Morgan is going to the Sanctuary. He needs one. He's mad, you know.

He's not going to the jail. Why go with him?

Sir says Morgan is all right to walk with and that Kate isn't to make a fuss. Kate was thinking that the thing most wrong with Morgan was how he wasn't in the two grades going to the city jail.

Of course he can't help that. Can't do a simple thing like murder somebody and get sent in jail. And of course he does think these funny things like the school is melting and Sir and the headmaster have to take him out.

But that was a long time ago. And Kate knew you can't tell what people are thinking until they say. We all know that.

It's hard to understand why he knew about Kate and the jail before she said it or did it.

She was thinking about the best thing on her map of the jail. Or she was nearly thinking about it. She was keeping it ready to think because it was so good. The best thing.

Better than Liza's scab. Kate followed that about all day but it stayed on, and Liza lost it at home during the night.

They went down to the station. Kate had worked it out. It was simple. And no one can tell what you are thinking. If you can't tell with Gwenda you can't tell with me.

If you can't tell with Morgan. But Morgan can't tell that he's thinking even when it's him. He can't tell from real. You can't tell with me, Kate.

You can't tell that when the top grades go across to the other platform Kate will be with them. She won't go on the train to the Sanctuary.

No way.

She will go to the jail. It isn't everybody that wants to, except the two top grades. Kate's train will go out of the station, over the bridge by the wharves, and down through the railway yards to the city.

The rest of the lower grades will go up the river and

cross it high up on the trestle bridge.

But Sir is waiting. Sir is out of sight, and Kate was running across with the two top grades. Leaving Morgan. He can think what he likes.

But Sir put out a hand and folded it on her shoulder. He brought her back.

He says he knows what she has been plotting and planning. But she is coming to the Sanctuary, and where is her coat and lunch?

And that is that. A train comes in on the other side of the rails. The two top grades wave from its windows.

Sir says Kate is to cheer up. What Kate thinks won't let her smile.

Then her train comes in. They get in it and go. Sir says he is going to stay at the Sanctuary when they get there. He was going to retire forty years early.

The train goes out of the station and up through the town.

It goes over the long trestle bridge. It gets out into the countryside.

Morgan pulls a map from his pocket. They are not on it yet. Kate pulls her map of the jail from her pocket. She is on it all the time.

When they get to the Sanctuary Morgan's map is not much use. It is an old one, and the animals have all walked into other enclosures. Morgan's brother Mel used the map years ago. It is broken down the middle. Morgan gets lost at once.

Kate relies on her map. For her it works. Those are not Emus. Those are The Governor and Mrs. Governor. That is not a Tree Kangaroo. That is a Trusted Prisoner. That is not the enclosure of the Dingoes. That is the Exercise Yard.

Sir wants to know whether it is good, eh?

Kate says it is right on. If you look close you can almost see the blood. Then Sir says he would like to look at her map. She shows him.

He thinks it is very helpful. To someone in the city jail.

He wants to find the way to the Lyrebird. Kate shows him the Jail Hospital. She wants to get there. They go there. It is full of Lyrebirds.

Next is a building called Morgue. Nothing to do with Morgan. Where they put dead prisoners. But where Kate is they keep Frogmouth Pipits in it.

But down in the city they keep Death Masks. They make lovely copies of the dead prisoners. If you go to the city jail you can see them.

Kate wanted to see them more than anything. It was the thought she had saved up. But she looked at the Tawny Pipit instead. It is feathers but looks like wood.

Then it begins to rain and she has no coat and no lunch.

People read your thoughts. Sir gives her a newspaper and twenty cents. The Death Mask Birds sit there in the rain.

CHAPTER 17

SWEET WATER RIVER

AN OLD, OLD woman. "Nothing ever happens these days," she said. "Not like when I was young."

Mel wondered how long it was since she was young. He often wondered about that when he saw her. Miss White was her name.

When she was young was about a hundred years ago, Mel thought. Of course nothing happened then. In those days they didn't know they were born. In fact most of them hadn't been born yet, all that time ago.

Of course she was right. Nothing ever happened these

days. Nothing much was happening now.

Mel and Joe were in River Street. It was O.K., nothing to rave about, watching the slab being poured on Mr. Young's new house. Mr. Young was there too, watching with the best, leaving the work to the men.

Miss White had come by. She wasn't watching the concrete going in. She was talking to Joe.

Joe reminded her of the old days. Joe reminded old people of the old days, way back before there was a proper town at Iramoo, before there was a bridge to the city side, when all travelers went by steamer. Before motorcars and trams.

Before bathrooms and water toilets. All these old people fascinated by dunnies and talking about them to Joe. Just because he was Chinese. Or something like that.

"One of you people used to have the night cart," said Miss White. Mel thought she was now talking about something else, not about nothing happening these days. But she was still talking about the same thing.

"I remember the night cart murder," she said.

"No you don't," said Mr. Young.

Everybody thought he had been leaning on the fence and thinking concrete. But he had been listening. He was the grandfather of Joe and really had something to do with the night cart business. Joe had nothing to do with it.

"You don't remember that," he said.

But of course if a person says they remember something then they must remember it. You forget or remember, thought Mel.

Mr. Young thought differently. Miss White said she certainly did remember. Mr. Young said she had heard a lot of talk about a murder. "But there never was one," he said.

The two oldies went on a bit about remembering and not remembering. They seemed to be forgetting what they were really talking about.

But it got a little clearer.

"They never found the body," said Mr. Young. "You can't have a murder without a body."

"Yes you can," said Miss White. "You could have burned someone up in your house when you set it on fire, and that would be murder without a body."

"If I killed them it would," said Mr. Young. "But the only person that got near killed was me. I was out in the back place. I forget it was the day."

Out in the back place, thought Mel. They don't think of anything else. It's unhealthy.

"What about the murder?" he said. "It sounds good."

"Good?" said Miss White. "It was terrible. The whole place stank."

"It was the rats," said Mr. Young. Mel thought it was the tallow factory that stank, because it still did. But they were meaning different things. Joe knew.

"Look," said Joe, "I keep hearing about all this. I just wish they'd all forget it."

"Rats?" said Miss White. "It was more than that. The night cart stopped coming, and the you-know-what didn't get taken away."

"Joe knows," said Mr. Young. "There were three sets of us on the night cart job. There was me, Lao Yung, with my father, and we had the dragon run. There was Cheng Li, and he had the snake run. There was Kai Thaw, and he had the rat. We put the names on the corners of the alleys and those were our places. We did the city and we did Iramoo."

"Nobody ever told me that," said Miss White. "I remember the boat in the Salt River. I was on it once when I fell off the steamer."

"I remember the foreign lady," said Mr. Young. "Nobody foreign any more, all same Australian. All same smell in boat."

"I don't remember you," said Miss White. "It was all young men in those days."

"All same young foreign lady," said Mr. Young. "I remember young lady. But I am Young now, change from Lao Yung."

Old Mr. Young, Mel thought. Old. But that's why she keeps talking to Joe. She thinks he's like his grandpa used to be. One day Joe will be a thousand-year egg like the old man. Another old Young.

"Did you empty ours?" said Miss White. She said her address.

But Mr. Young said he did not know. "All words gone

from back alleys," he said. "Don't know front of houses, only trapdoors at back, all by light of lantern."

"Go on about the murder," said Mel.

"They murdered each other," said Miss White. "Didn't you see it in the paper? It went on for such a long time."

"Kai Thaw," said Mr. Young. "Where is Kai Thaw? There was a bad time, but no murder. All poor people now. Poor but honest. One day there is a big rain, and the next day, and the next. Many days. Big lake at Salt River, all the way to city, no land, no trees. Big lake right across the park. Big high water all the way."

"All the streets were flooded," said Miss White. "We never got the salt damp out of the house."

"This was all sweet water," said Mr. Young. "Up, up, it comes. We have much difficulties in our job. You see, it is bad to get along the streets with the cart. It is hard for people to get across their yards. And then at the wharf where we load ship, the water too high and the boat too high and a long time loading. And then nowhere to unload. All this foreign dirt make good soil in our garden up the river. But all garden under water too. So a bad time for Lao Yung, Cheng Li, and Kai Thaw. We cannot do our job so we cannot be paid at the houses. We cannot bring vegetables down from our garden, so no money there. And our gardens wash away. Our boat is full so we cannot get our money. Our money is down in bottom of boat. Foreign devils do not look under that cargo. Not know good garden when they see

one, smell one. Now no good gardens, all dirt go to sea
and that is a bad way. Bad for sea, bad for land."

"All the same," said Miss White, "I remember that
a poor man was murdered."

"Not so," said Mr. Young.

Mel wished someone would start describing how the
murder had been done, and who had done it. Fancy,
he thought, the old man building a house with money
from those jobs.

"Old China way," said Mr. Young.

"Yes, it's a bit of a heathen custom," said Miss White.

Mr. Young went back to his story.

"That was the sweet water time," he said. "It was
bad. Worse was coming with the salt water. Rain, rain,
all day and night. Iramoo River rising up, all wash away.
Then a big tide up the Salt River. Kai Thaw on boat
one night. And when we come next day, no Kai Thaw."

"Murdered," said Miss White. "What did I tell you?
I remember it."

"You don't remember, it didn't happen," said Mr.
Young. "All same no boat too. Our dragon boat gone,
all gone, and our carts on the wharf, and nothing left.
We look in river, we look in marsh on city side. We
look everywhere. Then the policeman sees wife of Kai
Thaw. Then we go a long time in the city jail. Not speaking much Australian then, and getting to be hanged up
every day, we think. Cheng Li and I. But no boat, nowhere. Boat gone. Cargo gone. All money gone, all

gone. Two poor Chinamen, Cheng Li, Lao Yung come out of city jail."

"And then what?" said Miss White.

"Wifes and childs all dying out of hunger," said Mr. Young. "We go up-country a long time, working. We come back and find work here in ten, twenty years. But no boat. Down in bottom of river, by and by a piece comes up and another. But no murder, no Kai Thaw, no moneys, no boat, no dragon run."

"I'd prefer a murder," said Miss White. "Something has to happen some time. If it isn't going to happen now it must have happened then. What you say I don't care."

"Big truth," said Mr. Young. But he had told his story and was now watching the concrete again. It was still coming out like gray toothpaste, shiny and wet. "This reminds me," he said. "But better smell."

Miss White laughed. "It's my murder," she said to Joe. "I'll have to keep it."

"It's millions of years ago," said Joe. "I've heard it all before. I forget what everybody else thinks. Mel and I have been looking in the river for the boat, haven't we, Mel?"

"We've got a raft," said Mel. But he couldn't understand why Joe had not told him about the murder, all the same. He told Joe that, when Miss White had gone on down River Street.

"I can't remember what people know," said Joe. "Anyway, it isn't true. If I talk about it that makes my own grandfathers into murderers. No point in that. They've closed the city jail except for visitors. And they didn't do it. Anyway, like I said, I don't remember what you know. And it was millions of years ago."

"O.K.," said Mel. "But we still share the money if we find it."

Then another thought came to him.

"If he's a million years old already, why is he building another house at his age? Is he going to live another million years?"

"Yeah, it's no trouble to him," said Joe. "He does it all the time, don't you, Grandpa?"

"That's it," said Mr. Young. "It's cheaper than getting married again, and a lot quieter."

CHAPTER 18

FIRE ON THE WATER

"HE CAN TALK, can't you, beauty?" said Mary.

"That budgie just makes a noise," said Jack.

"He says, Poor Tom," said Mary.

"What's he say that for?" said Jack. "What does he want to say Poor Tom for? What's the meaning of that?"

"It means something to him," said Mary. "Or he wouldn't say it, would he?"

"I don't know," said Jack. "You say a lot of things that don't mean anything even to you."

"He says Poor Tom and he says Good Morning," said Mary. "Listen to him."

"You should get a chook," said Jack. "A chook is a poet against him. And you'd get an egg most days."

"Who's a good boy then?" said Mary.

"And what's more," said Jack, "who else in the world has a pure black budgie? There's something wrong with him."

"Black's very rare," said Mary.

"It wants to be," said Jack. "And he smells, too. Sort of smoky. He's got bad breath, that bird."

"Somebody's burning off," said Mary.

"More fool them," said Jack. "Won't get anything to burn in this weather. It's been raining five days."

"The river's up to the back fence," said Mary.

"What?" said Jack. "Why didn't you tell me when I came in? What's the good of telling me now?"

"What's the good of telling you at all?" said Mary. "You can't do anything about the river."

"I can go and look at it," said Jack. "But I'll feel a dill going out there at midnight. I can't do anything about it. Can I do anything about it, budgie?"

"Skwee," said the budgie. "Nup nup nup."

"All right," said Jack, "you put on your gumboots and go and have a look."

"Don't tease him, Jack," said Mary. "He understands. He's just trying to express himself."

"Put the cloth over him," said Jack. "I'm going to bed."

"You want a cloth over you sometimes, Jack," said Mary.

"I'll use my parka," said Jack. "I'll just take a turn down the yard and see what the river's doing."

"Don't worry," said Mary. "The river's never got in the house yet."

"First time for everything," said Jack. "O.K., I'll stay inside. If the water comes in the house that bird will give us a shout. Do you know what, covering it up hasn't made the smell any better."

"That's coming in from outside," said Mary. "Burning off."

"It's worse out here in the hall," said Jack. "And what a cold night. Did you put the electric blanket on?"

"Just after tea," said Mary. "It'll be right."

"You must have left the bedroom window open," said Jack.

"What?" said Mary. "I'm out in the kitchen. I can't hear you. What did you say?"

"I said the bedroom's full of smoke," said Jack. "Come here quick."

"Jack, what's all this smoke? I must put the budgie out in the kitchen, or it'll choke."

"Choke, smoke," said Jack. "The bed's on fire."

"Oh Jack," said Mary, "and on your side too. You'll

have to sleep in the spare room."

"Woman," said Jack, "if half the bed's on fire so is the other half. Pull out the plug, go on, pull it out. No, not the bath plug, the electric blanket plug."

"I'm getting some water," said Mary. "It's no good standing there and giving orders. That's no better than the budgie can do."

"I am not standing giving orders." said Jack. "I am picking up the covers from the bed and, and, blimey, they're hot. I'll put them in the bath."

"Then you'll want the plug in after all," said Mary.

"Now look," said Jack, "this is hopeless. What's all that in the bath?"

"That's my ferns," said Mary. "I brought them in to give them a drink."

"Brought them in to give them a drink?" said Jack. "It's been raining for five days."

"You're not supposed to water them from the top," said Mary. "You'd better put those covers out in the garden. The rain will put the fire in them out."

"Thanks," said Jack. "That's a girl, just push the screen door, will you?"

"Don't leave them on the veranda," said Mary.

"No way," said Jack. "Now we'd better get the mattress."

"There's just a little scorch on that," said Mary. "Not a lot."

"It's just the outside," said Jack. "But it's gone right through. I can see the springs inside. I can't see it burning, but that's what smells."

"Hurry out with it," said Mary. "I've got hold of my side of it."

"Easy does it," said Jack. "I don't think it will burst into flames."

"It's not that," said Mary. "I'm more worried about that poor bird choking in the smoke."

"Give it some beak-to-beak breathing," said Jack. "That'll waken it up. That'll make it lay eggs. Look, woman, don't let go your side of the mattress. We've got to get it outside."

"Jack, I'm opening the door so that we can do that," said Mary.

"Well, hurry up," said Jack. "I'm going to cough up an inner spring any minute now. I think I've got a lung on fire, just smoldering."

"That's your heartburn, Jack," said Mary. "You should take a tablet and lie down for a while."

"It wouldn't be my heart that was burning if I lay down on this mattress," said Jack. "It'd be my . . ."

"Don't you say anything vulgar, Jack," said Mary. "There, that's the door open."

"Blimey," said Jack, "we could leave the mattress here. There's enough rain coming in to put out ten of them."

"We can put this one out, and then the rain can put it out too," said Mary. "We can put the mattress out and the rain will put the fire out."

"They're the same thing," said Jack. "In this case. So don't split hairs."

"I'm not," said Mary. "This isn't a hair mattress."

"Never mind that," said Jack. "You just let it fall flat. I'll drag it across the veranda and put it in the garden."

"It seems a shame to get it wet, a good mattress like that," said Mary.

'I'll bring it in again if you like," said Jack. "But I think it would be a shame to burn the house down as well. You go in and water the budgie and give the ferns the kiss of death."

"There's no need to be nasty, Jack," said Mary. "Jack, what are you doing?"

"Nothing," said Jack. "Nothing at all."

"Where are you?" said Mary. "Jack."

"I'm just under the veranda," said Jack. "The whole garden is under two feet of water and I lost my footing and went into it."

"Jack, Jack, what shall I do?"

"Stand still, woman."

"But the mattress is starting to flame."

"But if you walk about you'll tread on my fingers again. I'm just holding on the edge of the veranda. I don't know how I got in here."

"Hurry up and come out," said Mary. "Or you'll be drowned and I'll be burned. It's great big flames."

"You should have kept the artificial respiration for the budgie," said Jack. "That isn't an inflatable bed. Now, here's the way out. Now what the devil are you doing, Mary?"

"All I'm doing is pushing the flaming mattress off the veranda into the floodwater," said Mary.

"Well you might gug gug gug than to put it gug gug gug when I'm gug gug gug," said Jack.

"Jack," said Mary. "Are you all right?"

"I'm fine," said Jack. "I wasn't going to stop talking just because you pushed my head underwater. It hasn't worked yet, and I don't suppose it ever will."

"No, I don't think it would," said Mary. "You'd talk through anything."

"There's some people could drown you with words," said Jack. "Come on, give us a hand."

"Why, Jack, you're all wet," said Mary.

"I've been under the water, remember," said Jack.

"I didn't think you'd gone right under," said Mary.

"This is the first time we've had a backyard pool," said Jack. "But you'll get used to people coming out of it wet, if it doesn't stop raining."

"Where's the mattress?" said Mary. "Did it go under the veranda too?"

"I hope not," said Jack. "What did you do, just push it in the water?"

"Yes," said Mary. "But I can't see it now."

"Get my flashlight," said Jack. "Go on, I'm too wet to be allowed in. It's in the kitchen. I'll stop here and get my death of cold. I will too, if she doesn't hurry back. Mary, come on."

"I was just having a look at budgie. He's all upset, sitting there in the dark and not knowing what's happening."

"Bring him out and let him have a look," said Jack. "If he fancies he's a duck. Give me the torch. There's the mattress, floating away."

"Jack, where's the back fence gone?"

"I expect it's still there," said Jack. "But under the water, that's all. Do you reckon the mattress is beyond it?"

"Yes," said Mary. "But, Jack, that's all river from our veranda edge as far as I can see."

"Right to the city, I daresay," said Jack. "But we've got a high veranda because it's a riverside block. It can't come up much further. But it's got rid of our mattress in a beaut way, carrying it off like that. Look at the smoke pouring from it. That'll go out to sea, no worries. Now go and get those ferns out of the bath, will you."

"They've been crying out for water, that's why they're there," said Mary.

"I'm sure I never heard them," said Jack. "You're enough talkers for me. I can't do with ferns shouting Water, water, but it might have been useful if the budgie had shouted Fire, fire, instead of muttering about Poor Tom."

CHAPTER 19

FLOODLIGHT

ALL THESE PEOPLE out at this time of night. In the dark, what are all these kids doing?

Coming to watch the flood rising. Coming to watch the Iramoo River fill up over its banks and come into the town.

Morgan to keep away from the edge, says his dad. Mel is to keep an eye on him. Mel can see Morgan's outside but not his inside. Morgan has all the water for miles around locked up in his mind.

The other people see it lying flat between the houses,

see it smooth between the stopped cars. Morgan sees the huge waves the water remembers. He sees the huge waves the water wants to be.

He sees them lifting higher and higher, over the houses, over the people. And they all go and live under it. Just Morgan, no worries with just Morgan.

And the sharks all up on the land. And the school up on the land, melting for real this time.

You could walk into the river, thinks Morgan.

No he doesn't, says his dad. Ought to be in bed.

You could tuck the sheets up so they don't get wet. A bed on the roof of the house.

Someone is talking about a bed. Not Morgan's dad, not Mel. Some other person. Morgan didn't think of it.

Kate says there must be someone in it. People smoke in bed. Morgan thinks she has strange thoughts. What bed?

A bed floating on the water.

Somebody in the bed.

Smoking.

Kate says of course it could happen. Shine your torch on it. Torches shine on it.

A mattress floating on the water. On the river. Smoke coming from it.

Wake them with an alarm clock. Tell them not to get out. It isn't a burglar under the bed. Only the river.

My river, Morgan thinks. All the rest of the world floating on top. Shouting at each other to wake up.

Smoking? Not smoking. On fire.

Fire. The river on fire. You have a fire to keep warm, even underwater.

The people on the mattress might be ill. The ill people lay dead. Dead? says Kate. Bring them in, the deathbed, the death sheet. Does anybody want them. I'll have them. I collect people, feathers, sharks, screams, ghosts. I am the collector. Bring them to me.

Lights on the water. Smoke going up. Kate wants the ashes. Morgan thinks about swimming under the bed. For him it is like walking is for others. No trouble.

Gwenda sees the mattress in the torchlight. She has a stone with her. Stones seem to grow where she is. In the middle of the divided highway she can find a stone.

Pluff, goes the stone. Something rises up in the bed on the water. Dust. Dust and ashes. And falls down again.

The people thought it was a reply from the sleepers. Some walk along the highway into the water. Someone thinks the bed is on top of a panel van stuck on the bridge. The bridge is under the water.

What crosses bridges under the water? Strange deep fish. No one could know. Morgan has a try at knowing. He thinks. He still cannot know.

The bed moves a little way down the river. It was not a panel van now.

Lightning, someone says. Lightning struck it. That is why it burns. Lightning has struck.

So it is the people burning the mattress, not the mattress burning the people.

Wet people in the road come back onto the land out of the river.

Sophia comes out of their house. Water is coming up out of the toilet. The wrong way round for things to go. Ivan and that family go to watch the water coming.

And the fish, Morgan thinks. A big eel. A big bottom-biting eel. Get Sophia.

Then the crowd is having a look at that, look at that, they are being told. The crowd is telling itself. What is it? Sophia coming out with a flood and a big eel?

Morgan swimming up a toilet out of the sea?

No. The river. The river in the middle. It has been flowing, flowing down. Down to the sea. All this water is river water, rainwater.

Now the river stops running. It stands still. It begins to lift up.

The sea is coming in. This is the Salt River. It has to have salt water in it. But for days and nights there has been sweet water.

Now the sea is coming back. The water is lifting higher. The crowd steps back, and steps back. A policeman steps back with it. In charge of the sea. May I see your license please, sea. Thank you. Stand over there, sea. Into the lockup, sea, into the city jail.

The tide, says the crowd. Lock up the tide too.

Wanted, one tide, medium build. Not very tall. With mustache and staring mad eyes, the demon tide.

The policeman tells Morgan to move back son. The tide gets away, the sea escapes.

The mattress stops going down the river. It stands on the tide. It stands there still lying down, not going anywhere. Still smoking. Who's driving this thing?

There should be some bones, thinks Kate. Cooked. I wonder whether you could eat them.

But they are going away. The mattress is going up on the tide.

Joe is watching. He has heard of floods before. He wonders where they have taken things, lost things. Where the flood of long ago took a boat. And a man. Lost things.

The mattress is like the boat. But mattresses sink. It stands to reason, they must. Not this one. Not a sensible mattress. Or not a sensible Joe to believe his eyes.

Mattress going upstream. Red glow of fire in it now. Whiff of smoke. Smell would drown a camel. Worse than the tallow factory.

Where will it go? Joe is not the only one to ask. There is the boy Dee, Kate's brother. Where is it going he asks, without saying a word. Joe does not know, without saying a word.

Mel comes up a little way and wonders about the same thing. Joe says he is going to find out.

Gwenda has stones she wants to throw. Kate wants the bones. Morgan comes with Mel. Morgan does not care about things in the same way as others. They are all strange to him. If he wanted. If he wanted he could just walk out there, on top, not swimming, and look at the bed, the mattress, the people in it.

Sit there beside them on the water like glass.

Instead he goes with the others along the edge of the park. They push through shrubs and trees. Morgan knows they are iron, you can't move them, not a leaf of them. The river is glass, the park is iron.

The others tear themselves to bits on the leaves. Like running through knives. All their blood goes up in the sky, they fall down, there is just Morgan, Morgan, everywhere.

Then he catches up with them. Iron bends, of course. Blood running up, blood running down.

They cross the park and go up the riverbank. Out on the water the bed floats quiet. A square hole in the water, the chimney of an underwater fire.

They can see it clearly now. Daylight is coming. Far off in the towers of the city the lights go up.

Mel and Joe climb up beside the trestle bridge, lift the wire for the rest. The quiet shining rails lie wet. The bed goes under the bridge.

And then the water has risen high enough to flow over in a place only water could see. Water with the eye of the sea. Salt water like tears running down a new place. The dip in the bank of the river sucking the sea in on a paddock. And sucking the bed across with it.

And the drinking stops. The water stops. The river runs down again. The tide has turned. It has escaped from its jail.

The bed stops on the slope of the paddock. There is no one in it but a round hole with burning edges. Nothing.

Gwenda kicks it. Kate sees its own springy skeleton. Morgan smiles back at its mouth. Dee says he has to get home. Mel and Joe agree.

They all go home on the raft belonging to Joe and Mel. They get a dink down on it. Morgan goes to sleep. He can't tell which he is. His life goes on in dreams as well. Kate is hungry. Any warm bones would have done. Gwenda throws a stone at the trestle bridge and hits it, ding.

CHAPTER 20

THE TRESTLE BRIDGE

MR. OLANIK WAS polishing a brass pipe on his old retired railway engine. He was in the shed at the bottom
of his yard where the engine was kept.

"No," he said. "You cannot use it." He was talking to
Mel and Joe. He was talking to Kev as well, but Kev
was outside the building talking to a cat.

Mr. Olanik's grandson Dee was there too. Mel and
Joe and Kev would rather be without Dee. But they
wanted the use of the engine for an hour or two, so they

had had to find Dee and bring him along.

"It's my grandpa's boat," said Joe. "About a hundred years ago it got lost. We just found it the other day up by the trestle bridge. It got out of the river in a flood and over in a paddock and fell nearly to bits. We want to pull it back in the river."

"It's Kev being such a dill gave us the idea," said Mel. "He said tie it on the end of a train and that would pull it to the river. Then we remembered you."

"And as well, remember, they have taken up the line. I cannot get the engine out on the State railway lines now. So that is all," said Mr. Olanik. "That is all," and he put the lid back on his metal polish.

That was that, it seemed.

"We brought about half a ton of briquettes," said Mel. "To make the fire."

Mr. Olanik gave a last wipe to the pipe and said nothing.

So they left him. They left the great heap of briquettes too. They wandered down the line in the cutting at the end of the yard. At the end of the cutting the lines had been pulled up and laid to one side. And there was a firm new wire fence.

"Heave ho, one two three," said Kev. He thought he would lift a rail and put it back in place. It was a short rail, anyone could move that, he thought.

It was a short rail weighing four hundred and fifty

kilos. You have to lift all the kilos at once, of course. If you are Kev you don't move any of them. If you are Kev and Mel you don't lift any. If you are Kev, Mel, Joe, and Dee you move it along a bit, but not up at all.

Mr. Olanik had walked down behind them. "Go home, boys," he said. "And that is not the way to do it. You see it is simple when you know."

He knew. He showed them. He found two metal bars lying about in the railway yards beyond the fence. With them he levered the rail, and by himself he could make it move. With them all helping they could easily put the rail where they wanted.

"Just a lesson," said Mr. Olanik. "We are not doing it. Boys, boys, stop it at once."

But no one could stop. Mr. Olanik could not let go, could not leave them. "A bit more along, to the side, down, out round, away, wide, close, up, and there, that is her place. But she will not run on one rail, so quick now with the other. And over, through, heave, under, by, aside, over, back, in, and there, she is in, and now the spikes and the fishplates, and that is a rail."

"Now the engine," said Dee. "Come on, Grandad."

"Never," said Mr. Olanik. "Stop it, boys, go away. It is a quiet Sunday, you should be at home doing good things."

"Better the day better the deed," said Kev.

And "Go home, boys," was what Mr. Olanik said all

the rest of the afternoon. While they lit the fire in the
engine, filled it with water, greased every bearing, loaded
the box with briquettes, sorted out a long piece of chain
and two others, put on board a key for altering the points
along the State railway system.

"And what else I do not know for our nights in the
city jail," said Mr. Olanik.

"No one will see us," said Joe.

"If we are not going we are not being seen," said Mr.
Olanik. "That is being best."

"We're going," said Mel.

"Mad," said Mr. Olanik. "City jail is too good for us."

They went. Pressure came up on the dial. Heat rose
from the funnel, from the boiler. Steam came out under
the wheels. Reflections moved in the polished brass pipes,
little skies and tiny trees. The engine was out of its shed
and ran down the cutting.

At the end they shifted the fence to one side. Then
slowly crossed the new-laid lines.

"Derailing is coming," said Mr. Olanik. But it did not.

They were free in the big yard behind the Iramoo
station.

"Some job getting across to the main lines this is,"
said Mr. Olanik. "You get lost alone, or I leave you now.
I take you over."

They went a zigzag course up and down the comb of
lines, crossing over at the points, running this way and

that, until they came out at the end of the station platform.

No one was there.

"No trains until seven o'clock," said Mr. Olanik. "We
end by then, no worries."

"Right on," said Kev. And forgot about being quiet
and blew the whistle.

"They hear the train blow," said Mr. Olanik. "Hush."

No one called. No one came. No one had heard, perhaps.

Now the engine was on the open line. They ran up
behind the houses in a long soft curve and over to one
side of them the trestle bridge began to appear.

"The quarter mile we call it in my time," said Mr.
Olanik. "Now they have kilometers again, not so good."

The line curved still, coming through paddocks and
new building lots. Then the bridge pulled round and
pulled round until it opened up ahead of them.

"There, now," said Joe. "Stop."

"We could run to the city," said Mr. Olanik. "She is
going best, don't you think, boys?"

"Great," said Mel. "But stop."

"Boys, boys," said Mr. Olanik. "First you bring me
out all wrong, and then you stop me. It is wrong."

But he stopped the engine at the end of the bridge,
where the firm ground became the hollow ground of the
bridge deck.

Away down the river people were watching. From the edge of the park.

"Kids," said Mel. He jumped down with the end of the chain. You have to drag chain because of the weight. But it is easier than a solid rail because you can lift some of it and get hold, or move a bit of it at a time.

Mel went down the bank into a paddock. On the bank there was something of wood. It had been made up into an object at one time. But that had been a hundred years ago, Joe said.

A hundred years ago it had been a boat. His grandfathers' boat. Two grandfathers, who had used it for their market garden trade. Now it was washed up, lost, out of the river. You could only tell it was a boat by knowing that the carved dragon at the stern of it was what the lost boat had had. The rest was buried, rotted, burned, broken.

The chain went on a clear good ring that Mel and Joe had found when they were digging round.

"What is making you look here?" said Mr. Olanik to Dee.

"He doesn't know," said Joe. "We were following a burning mattress up the river during the floods last week, and it got over the bank just here and stopped just there. So we thought about it and came and looked again. And there was the boat we lost in the flood a hundred years ago."

"And now," said Mr. Olanik. "Are you ready for pulling?"

"Yes," said Joe. "We dug all round it. It's too heavy to move, that's all."

"It will sink," said Mr. Olanik. "You will blame me."

"It'll be right," said Joe. "Pull."

The engine moved onto the bridge. The chain lifted itself up a link at a time, hanging and hanging and then a long curve, and the long curve straightening. It was a bar of metal now.

"Stand back," said Mr. Olanik. And they all waited for something to break.

Nothing broke. The boat seemed to heave itself up, as if it were alive, a hippopotamus coming out of the mud. It came up out of the place where it lay and slid up the grass to the top of the riverbank.

Then the chain caught on the support of the bridge, and Mr. Olanik stopped the engine and went back.

This time Mel put the chain out between the supports and there was another pull. The boat tipped itself and began to slide down the bank.

Mr. Olanik could see what was happening and went on pulling. There was going to be trouble if he did it wrong. If the boat went down and pulled the chain tight between it and the engine and caught the end of the bridge too, then they might never get loose.

But Mr. Olanik left enough at the top for him to stop

the engine, get down and fasten the chain against the bridge, run the engine back a little to slacken the chain between it and the fastening, and then knock out the fastening. The chain fell down from the bridge onto the boat, and all the pulling was done, and the engine was free.

The next hard work was getting the chain up again, all its length and all its weight.

"Good-bye, and thanks a million," said Mel to Mr. Olanik. "You going on to the city then?"

"Boys, boys," said Mr. Olanik. "I do all this work for you, and you must come back and put away the engine, that is the least."

"Yes, come on," said Dee. It wasn't up to him to speak to them like that, but he was right.

"I'll just keep guard," said Kev. "Sit on it, like."

But when he thought he would go down to the boat he looked and decided he wouldn't.

Because now, now that the boat had been moved and shaken and stirred there could be plainly seen in it the shape of bones.

Not animal bones. But the shape of a man's skull.

"What are you finding?" said Mr. Olanik. "Boys."

"That's all right," said Joe. "It's beaut. That's Kai Thaw. He got lost with the boat all that time ago. They thought Cheng Li and Lao Yung had murdered him. But here he is. Cheng Li is Mr. Lee now, and Lao Yung is Mr. Young. And now we have Kai Thaw and the boat."

Mr. Olanik went home alone, puffing and steaming. Dee should have gone with him, the others thought, but he did not, so here he was with them. Not very much wanted, but there.

The next bit they did themselves. They pushed the boat into the water, complete with its bony crew.

It floated. Joe stayed with it a little while and the others went down to get the raft.

So it was Joe that saw the bubbles rise through the rubbish in the bottom of the boat. And the water after the bubbles. And then saw the waters rising like a flood again up the sides of the old planking. Or perhaps the boat was sinking.

So when the others got back he was holding only the dragon carved on the stern, and the rest had gone.

They towed a submerged wreck down to the Iramoo wharves and tied up at a vacant berth.

The next thing they did not see. On Monday Mr. Young and Mr. Lee came down and rented the berth, as they used to so many years before. They raised the remains of the boat, and took out of it what they wanted.

"It is ours," they said. "Kai Thaw we shall bury. The rest we shall keep. It is worth very little now."

Because there had been treasure in the boat. Money. Guarded so many years by the dead Kai Thaw.

It was enough to buy Mel and Joe and Kev, and Dee though no one wanted him, a meal at the Chinese restaurant owned by a cousin of Joe's.

Mr. Olanik put the rails to the side of the track, ran his engine home. Then he waited for the State railways to come and have strife with him. No one came. No one had seen.

"Boys," he said, when he saw them, "it is worse than if they are coming. If you have a wife you fear the mother-in-law, and if you have a railway engine you fear the State law. I am thinking life is not meant to be easy."

CHAPTER 21

STAR OF THE IRAMOO

KATE WAS ANGRY. She was worse than that, she was wild. She was more than that, she was mad. She was out of her skull.

She really was.

"You mean," she said to Dee, "you mean you had some bones in your hand and you never gave them to me?"

"Right," said Dee. "They were someone else's bones."

"No use to him," said Kate. "You know I want bones

more than anything else in the world."

"Yeah, so does everyone," said Dee. "Except slugs and things, and they've got a different system."

"And I'd give anything for a skull," said Kate. That was the skull she was out of. "Anything I'd give."

"You haven't got anything," said Dee. "So hard cheese."

"I deserve a bone," said Kate. "I'll never be a great collector unless I have some human bones."

"You would have human bones if you were a human," said Dee. "A whole set."

"Hmm," said Kate. She went off in her rage to find Gwenda. Gwenda would probably find her a human skull one of these days. Most likely Sophia's, and very likely cracked by Gwenda.

Gwenda did not want another human skull. Or any bones of people. If she saw one floating in the river, she said, she would throw stones at it. Practice against Sophia.

They found Sophia and took her along with them. Not out of kindness, but in case they didn't find anything better.

Said Gwenda. She took some stones with her.

"And there was treasure too," said Kate. Dee had found bones and treasure. Enough treasure to give him and his friends a whole meal.

"Probably going to have one every year forever," said Kate. "I didn't get invited."

They went down to the Salt River. That was the place for skulls and treasure, Kate said.

You get them both together. You don't have to learn that, you just know it, and it comes true.

Gwenda thought she might keep the treasure. She could manage with the skulls she had. Kate thought that the treasure should be shared, at least.

Gwenda threw a stone or two at a floating bottle. Then she got angry because she hit it and it broke. The stupid thing sank.

Sophia did a nice thing for Gwenda. She found a piece of wood and threw that in for Gwenda to throw her stones at.

Gwenda said she wasn't a dog, doing tricks. Sophia couldn't please her. That was a rule of life, like skulls and treasure going together.

Sophia had to throw her own stones at the piece of wood. Gwenda stood by and told her how badly she did it. Sophia used up all her small stones.

But they thought they would move on, because now they were under the wall of the tallow factory. You can get used to the smell most of the time, but now and then you think you'll get sick.

You wonder what they did in there. Kate wasn't sure what a tallow was, Gwenda thought it was a fat animal, all fat.

Sophia dug out a round stone and threw it at her piece of wood.

She was a rotten thrower. No idea, said Gwenda. And the stone landed in front of Gwenda and splashed up all that black Salt River mud. Gwenda picked the stone up out of the mud and got ready to throw it back.

She didn't throw it quite at once. She thought Sophia was too near. Gwenda liked to hurt you, but she liked to use her skill as well. Her skill was throwing and hitting, and there is not much skill in throwing at someone near enough to touch.

Sophia had even less skill. She had thrown the stone and dropped it as near she could have put it.

"Run," said Gwenda.

Sophia thought she would stay where she was. And Gwenda thought the stone was a bit too big. She actually had a sort of rule about not killing anyone. It was a rule she had just broken and got cross about. She had broken a floating bottle without meaning to. Now she might kill Sophia without meaning to. She would rather have gone on torturing the bottle, and torturing Sophia.

"Can't even run," she said. "You can stay then."

But she was interested in the stone. She was going to throw it in the water just for the splash. But it was so smooth and round and felt as if it should be shining. But it wasn't shining. It was covered with Salt River slimes and muds.

"Do tallows have skulls?" said Kate.

"Yes," said Gwenda. That solved the smooth stone.

It was the skull of a tallow. It could just be. If no one knows what a tallow is they can't say it isn't the skull of one.

"Catch," said Gwenda. She threw gently. Kate dropped the stone.

"What is it?" she said. "A big water-lolly?"

"One of your skulls," said Gwenda. "Let's go on up the park, now we've found that."

But Kate had to kneel down and rinse the stone. It felt strange to her as well. It was too smooth and the wrong heaviness.

It came out of the water shining, but only with being wet and clean. You couldn't have ever seen your face in it, or anything like that.

"It isn't a skull," said Kate. "Skulls have eyes. That's why I want one."

"You can have it all the same," said Gwenda. "I just want the treasure bit of what we find."

"It might be," said Kate.

Gwenda dug up a piece of mud and threw it up into the air. She knew what she was doing. It landed on the window of the tallow factory, splat. It hung there and slid down and dirty water ran from it.

"The flying cow strikes again," she said. She said things like that.

"I think it's an opal," said Kate.

"Opals are like red and green jellies mixed," said

Gwenda. "That looks like mud and mud mixed."

"You've got to open them up," said Kate. "Sort of like getting the brains out."

"Opals are valuable," said Sophia. "Worth a lot of money. But money isn't worth very much these days," she added, when Gwenda looked at her with disgust.

"It's a real big one," said Kate. "They get special names, and this one's the Star of the Iramoo. When I've got it up I'll wear it round my neck."

"You'll sell it," said Gwenda. "How do you open it?"

"It's jewels," said Kate. "A jewel man will do it."

Then a door opened in the factory wall above them.

"Got you," said a man. His name was Jack. "You chucking mud on our windows?"

"Us?" said Gwenda.

"That's right, you with the mud on your hands," said Jack.

"It was the flying cow," said Gwenda.

"Striking again," said Kate.

"What have you got there?" said Jack. "A stone all ready to throw."

"No," said Sophia. "An opal."

"You should be so lucky," said Jack. "Don't get many opals in this river. Give it here."

"I'll hold it and you can look at it," said Kate. "Then we're going to sell it."

"I found it," said Sophia. "I had it first."

"Then it can't be an opal," said Gwenda. "No way."

"No, that's not an opal," said Jack. "I promise you it isn't an opal. You'll find some more of these about down there. It's just as interesting as an opal, and it might be more rare. More opals about than these."

"Diamond," said Kate. "Or a skull."

"No, you'd never guess," said Jack. "This is a stone out of the stomach of a horse. They grow in there in some horses. I've seen them as big as your head. They just grow in their stomachs."

"And it kills them," said Gwenda.

"No," said Jack. "Doesn't do any harm. But that's what that is. They call them bezoar stones."

"No treasure," said Gwenda.

"Not nice, out of insides," said Sophia.

"Perfect," said Kate. "Not quite so good as a skull from somebody. But a stone out of an animal. I reckon that's a beaut thing. Grouse. Can I keep it?"

"Don't put it in your mouth, you'll swallow it," said Jack. "No use to anyone. You keep it."

Kate went straight home.

"You move on too," said Jack to Gwenda and Sophia.

Kate washed the stone from the stomach of the horse. It was the most beautiful thing in her collection. There were more beautiful things to be got, one day, like skulls from people. But the stone was good.

In Gwenda's pocket were stones she liked just as well but wouldn't keep.

"We'll go up the park," she said to Sophia. "I'll give you a swing."

Sophia said yes. She had forgotten that when she was helpless on the swing Gwenda would throw stones at her, for practice.